Dedicated to the men and women who courageously move forward after an abusive relationship, and to the people who help them heal.

To my husband, Joe—
I'm grateful for the all ways you make me feel consistently loved, valued, and cherished.
Thank you.

THE
PAIN
BEHIND
THE
PORTRAIT

JENELL HOLLETT

The Pain Behind The Portrait is a work of fiction.
Names, characters, and incidents are a product of imagination.
Any resemblance to actual persons, living or dead, or events, past or present, is entirely coincidental.

ISBN: 1503391388
ISBN 13: 9781503391383
Library of Congress Control Number: 2014921324
CreateSpace Independent Publishing Platform
North Charleston, South Carolina

Acknowledgements

First, a huge thanks to all of you who purchase and take the time to read this book. Without you, all the work of researching and writing would seem empty. Your comments and online reviews are important to authors and I want to personally thank you for taking the time to read and respond.

It would have been impossible to get inside Mike's mind without the invaluable help of my husband, Joe. Whenever I asked, Joe would share his take on the male viewpoint, usually with the comment "A man would look at it like this…" or "A guy wouldn't say that." I am grateful to have a husband who encourages my writing and willingly shares his insight and perspective.

My friend Scott Charlton did an incredible job editing the first manuscript. He generously shared his time and expertise, asking only for a signed copy in return. Scott's suggestions, perspective, and eye for typos significantly improved this manuscript and strengthened Mike's voice and descriptions. Thank you so much, Scott. You are a gifted editor.

Vicente "Vee" Ramos, my friend and graphic designer, helped me determine the best cover for this novel. His artistic talent and attention to detail astound me. I am grateful for the outstanding work and personal service I consistently receive from everyone at Minuteman Press, Encinitas. My heartfelt thanks for all the successful projects and fun times that have resulted from our collaboration.

My team at CreateSpace, particularly Rebecca, Colleen, and Lance, went the extra mile to assure this book was completed with professionalism and quality. Publishing a book is always a circuitous journey, so I'm grateful for the personal attention and kindness I've received from these individuals. Thank you. It's a privilege to recommend CreateSpace to other authors.

Shyanne Smith, my friend and executive coach, has believed in this book from the beginning. When she read the manuscript her words were "The world needs this book." Her excitement propelled my writing and kept me focused even when I was buried in things like home renovation and caring for my mother. Thank you Shyanne, for guiding me to a place of determination and purpose, and for showing me the value of being a tug boat in the literary world of ocean liners.

My cherished friend and prayer partner Charlotte Jordan opened my mind to the idea of becoming an author. Every book I write is a direct result of her encouragement, belief in me, and continual prayers on my behalf.

Michelle Haneline and Kathy Jordan are always the first to volunteer to read my next book. Ana Chota encourages and inspires me. Girlfriends like these are valuable beyond measure, not just for their wisdom, but also for their honesty and right-on-the-mark advice.

My world is richer and my writing more authentic because I am blessed with a vast and rich network of family and friends. My mother Ruth, our kids, Carina, Claire, Brent, and Melissa, sons-in-law Roger and Pat, and granddaughter Riley are my inner circle of support and love. My brother Bradley, my second family the Loders, my large extended family, my friends, and my church family are generous in their support of my writing and are consistently there in times of joy or difficulty. My heartfelt thanks to all of you for the many ways you support and encourage my writing and speaking career.

Albert, my friend in Escondido, Sherrie, my classmate in Tennessee, Dianne, my classmate in Pismo Beach, Raquel, my friend in Carlsbad, and Pam, my classmate in Murrietta—thank you for helping me promote my writing and speaking career. You're like my own PR team! Your support and excitement inspires me and makes me smile when I think about you.

Above all, I am grateful to God for my innate writing and speaking abilities. These are unearned gifts and I am humbled by the realization God entrusted them to me. I pray I use them to His glory.

Introduction

"Verbal abuse is the use of words to cause harm to the person being spoken to. It is difficult to define and may take many forms. The harm caused is often difficult to measure.

"The most commonly understood form is name-calling. Verbal abuse may consist of shouting, insulting, intimidating, threatening, shaming, demeaning, or derogatory language, among other forms of communication...

"Victims of verbal abuse are often told they are to blame for the abuser's behavior and reluctant to take action to end the abuse."

—www.USLegal.com

"In a verbally abusive relationship, the partner learns to tolerate abuse without realizing it and to lose self-esteem without realizing it."

—**Patricia Evans,** *The Verbally Abusive Relationship: How to recognize it and how to respond*

"Words can be said in bitterness and anger, and often there seems to be an element of truth in the nastiness. And words don't go away, they just echo around."

—**Jane Goodall**

vii

1

WRITTEN ONE MONTH AFTER OUR FIFTEENTH WEDDING ANNIVERSARY AND PUT IN A DRAWER

They say you marry your unfinished business. If that is true—and from my experience it must be—then I walked down a path created by my father and fell over a cliff into the arms of my wife. She is exquisite and well regarded and mercurial, my wife—a goddess directly from the pages of Greek mythology. She is beauty and rage, loveliness and cruelty. I am her human foil, the recipient of her moods and her flashes of anger toward all men.

Our house, high on the hills overlooking the Pacific Ocean, is decorated in designer colors and rich fabrics that remind me of the vibrant colors in a forest. There are deep reds and warm golds with touches of green and blue. My wife is skilled at finding key pieces that turn a room from ordinary to stunning. But in spite of the warm colors and well-placed pieces, there is a cold formality to our home that subtly informs guests to avoid stain-inducing behaviors and never place their feet on the furniture.

A formal portrait of our family hangs above the fireplace so everyone who enters can see the beautiful family of four. I look at the picture every evening when I come home exhausted, anxious to move my legs and stretch the muscles of my back. My wife, Dayne, is the center of the portrait. Her red dress dips low in the front, revealing the cleavage that brought me to my knees. Her green eyes look directly at the camera, and her long dark lashes and red lips are inviting. She is a beautiful woman on the outside, and most men believe I am a lucky man. I believed that for a short time after our wedding, but then I began to understand the emptiness of a marriage to a beautiful woman who can never be satisfied.

Standing slightly behind Dayne is our son, Matt. The picture was taken two months after his tenth birthday. He will grow to be tall and broad shouldered, but in this picture his face still has the soft edges of a boy. His brown hair is short and spiked, a style he has favored since he joined the swim team and hair became unimportant. At the photographer's directive, Matt's hand rests on his mother's shoulder in a show of solidarity that belies the reality of their growing distance. Dayne will tire of Matt when he becomes a teenager and shows signs of being a man someday. They will fight the entire week he turns thirteen and gradually learn to avoid one another.

I stand between Matt and MarLea, our daughter. She was seven in this picture, innocent but self-protective, in awe of her brother and watchful of her mother's temper. In the picture she is leaning slightly against my side, and I have my arm wrapped protectively around her shoulders. Her red dress is soft and her light brown hair is full of soft curls that, if my memory serves me well, smelled floral and innocent. MarLea looks like her mother. Fortunately the similarities are only skin-deep. My daughter is kindhearted and vulnerable, tender yet strong. She inherited my love of music, although she chose to play the guitar rather than the piano, the instrument that showed me what notes on a page can accomplish and introduced me to Saint-Saëns and Beethoven, Dave Brubeck and Diana Krall. Now that she's older, sometimes in the evenings, MarLea will come down to my study in her drawstring pajamas and read in the overstuffed chair while I check my e-mail or work on a contract. My study is our hideaway, and we surround ourselves with music from my iPod so no other sounds can penetrate. Dayne hates classical music, so MarLea and I make our musical choices based on whether we need relief from Dayne's moods. If Dayne is happy, we may choose jazz or soul or rock. If Dayne is angry, we will always choose classical.

I am also in the picture. *Present* is the word I would use. I was present at the portrait appointment, as if I were the family pet. I made no decisions, had no input. I simply showed up. If you know me well, you can see that in my face. The man standing in the family portrait does not have the same excitement in his eyes that invigorated his high school football pictures. He does not have the outgoing, easy smile you can see in his college photos. He does not even show the cockiness of his law school graduation picture. He is just present, a successful hood ornament precisely positioned in order to demonstrate family unity and status. It's a large expensive portrait that is a photographer's fantasy, a one-page novel hanging above our fireplace. That beautiful unified family does not exist. It never did.

Tonight I am sitting at my desk working. Dayne is not here. Matt is away at college, and MarLea is upstairs working on homework. It's a typical night in our house. We are each alone in the world.

3

2

OUR HONEYMOON

I wrote those words on a night when the moisture of the Pacific Ocean blanketed our neighborhood with coastal fog. Sleep evaded me, so I crawled quietly out of bed at two in the morning and returned to the safety of my office. That page about my marriage was a practice piece. I thought if I could master the art of descriptive writing, maybe one day I might actually craft a well-written novel. But that hasn't happened. I run out of adjectives and then I run out of confidence. Maybe one day I will write my novel, but for now I've decided to write for therapy...to share the pain of my marriage and the detours I never expected my life to take. I'm writing because there's no one to talk to anymore. My wife responds to my attempts at conversation with denunciations and reprimands. My friends have their own challenges and don't need to hear mine. So I'm letting the paper absorb all the pain, anger, and frustration I need to expel. Believe me, it needs to come out, or it's going to do damage.

My marriage is dead. I wear the burial mask on my face every day. I've managed to create a mask that's amazingly lifelike. Maybe writing will help me move from a place of sadness and plastered facial expressions to a place of acceptance. I suppose to make that journey, I have to start from the beginning...my early years with Dayne.

I have fond memories of those early days. Some were blissful, but in retrospect I realize the bliss was often accompanied by a sharp, uncomfortable

5

jolt. Now that I look back, I can see those jolts were indicators of fault lines below the surface, the tectonic plates of our life colliding, shifting, causing friction. I didn't understand then, but I do now. Those fault lines eventually cause irreversible seismic shifts. But it's hard to see such large life movements from the perspective of early love.

I remember our honeymoon. I awoke the first morning to a brilliant blue sky and the sound of Hawaii's waves beyond our open patio door. Dayne was asleep, her dark hair falling across the pillow and her mouth slightly open. She was beautiful even in sleep, and I was filled with a renewed excitement to be her husband. After three years of living together, waiting for me to finish law school and scrape together the money to afford the wedding of her dreams, we married. I thought perhaps her parents would help with the wedding, but five years before they had invested in a sure thing that turned out to be a Ponzi scheme, so they had nothing to share from their nonexistent savings and a decimated retirement account. My parents were capable of helping with the wedding, but when I asked him, my father's words were, and I quote, "You gotta lot of nerve thinking I'm going to pay for something her cheap-assed parents should be taking care of. What kinda white-trash gal are you marrying?" Needless to say, I paid for the wedding. It's still a little puzzling to me that Dayne, knowing I was paying for the entire thing only one year out of school and at least half on credit cards, insisted on a $3,000 wedding dress, but at the time I thought—she's my fiancée. She's entitled to all the beautiful things I can provide for her.

That morning we planned to snorkel at Place of Refuge. I'd done my homework, read the AAA Hawaii guidebook, and made the reservations. We were scheduled to meet the zodiac boat at ten that morning, so I curled up next to Dayne and gently stroked her hair. She moved slightly then reached for my face. Her hand was soft as she moved it across my cheek and down my chest and stomach. I knew by her touch she wanted me. We made love slowly, and afterward she lay beside me with her face nestled against my shoulder, the warmth of her body a sharp contrast against the cool breeze. I was such a happy man—a happily married man. I glanced at the clock and realized we had only fifteen minutes to dress and get to the boat. We were laughing as we rushed around the room, throwing items into the backpack. We arrived exactly at ten. Dayne took my hand and snuggled against me after we completed the forms and sat on a bench waiting for the boat.

Suddenly, without warning, her mood changed. She stiffened a bit, sat up a little straighter, a little farther from me. I reached over to put my arm around her, mistakenly thinking she might be cold.

"It feels funny to write Dayne Passick on the form," she said to me.

"Really?" I reply. "Why?"

"I just think Passick is a weird name. I probably should have kept my maiden name. I don't know if I like the sound of Dayne Passick. And, can you not sit so close? Your hairy arm keeps tickling me."

I was stunned and too startled to answer. I didn't insist she take my name. She knew my last name was Passick from the beginning. If she wanted to stay Bailey, that was all right with me. I didn't know what to say or do, so I sat silently for a minute.

"Our kids will probably get teased a lot. You know...kids can be so cruel when you have a stupid last name," she whispered a little too loudly.

"Yeah," I said, trying not to sound defensive. "I adjusted to those lame jokes. Our kids will adjust."

The boat arrived and we settled onto the inflated side. After a few minutes, Dayne put her hand on my thigh and squeezed. "Can't wait to be back at the room tonight," she said seductively. She was back to the happy newlywed. I smiled at her instinctively amid my tumbling thoughts.

We bounced along the top of the waves for twenty minutes, constantly adjusting our position to keep from falling out of the boat. The zodiac slowed and turned sharply into a cove surrounded by jagged volcanic rock and tall green palms. No wonder we couldn't access this easily from the land. This coast was unfriendly from that angle, but beyond the crashing waves and sharp rocks, the ocean was accessible if you chose to enter on her terms.

Dayne and I snorkeled among brightly colored fish while turtles glided effortlessly through the water. The sun was warm, the water cool. We held hands as we floated on the swells and then dived to mimic a fish or turtle that swam by at a safe distance. We took pictures with our disposable underwater camera and realized when we picked up the prints two week later that the only ones worth saving were the pictures of us. The colors of the fish and coral looked bland and faded in the pictures. They were hardly worth saving.

Within a year, I realized the bliss in my marriage had begun to fade too. But it seemed like a normal occurrence at the time. You can't honeymoon forever.

3

THE EARLY YEARS

My father was a formidable man, both in business and in his own home. By today's standards he was abusive, but in those days they called it keeping your kids in line. He rarely hit us. He didn't need to—his words were punishment enough.

Our mother was a consistent, capable woman. My brother and I obeyed her from a deep foundation of mutual respect and because, even at a young age, we felt connected to her as recipients of my father's vitriolic tongue. All of us—my mother, my brother, Paul, and I—lived in a state of crushing confusion and defensive posture. We didn't understand how my father's emotions could turn so quickly. One moment his tone would be kind and the next, like a rogue wave, his words would slam into our unprotected shores and demolish the small sand castles of self-worth we'd been struggling to build.

Sadly, my mother believed most of what our father said about her. When he said, "You're lucky I married you, because you would have been a pathetic old maid without me," she believed she could not have done any better than to marry him. When my father said, "It's a good thing I don't have a wandering eye with all the attention I get at work. Lucky I'm sticking around here because without me you'd have nothing," she believed if he ever left her, she would be destitute. When he told her she was lucky to have married up, she believed him. My father's family owned two grocery

9

stores and took vacations to Niagara Falls and Yellowstone. My mother's parents worked for minimum wage. She rode the bus to secretarial school and worked two jobs to help feed her younger brothers and sisters.

I neither fully believed nor fully disbelieved my father. He was an unpredictable force in my childhood, and I lacked the necessary skills to deal with such uncertainty. My brother distanced himself as soon as possible, but I tried for most of my elementary years to find a pattern, to predict my father the way a meteorologist predicts hurricanes. The more I tried, the more confused I became; so little about my father's behavior made sense to me. It was hard for me to accept that my father, the man who brought gifts home from business trips, who lovingly assembled our bicycles and built us a tree house, who wrapped his arms around my mother's waist as she stood over the kitchen sink, was the same man who made me cry into my pillow so many nights, hurting in both body and soul.

"I should have used a condom and saved myself the trouble of having you, boy," he would bark at Paul when report cards arrived. "You're stupid. Look at these grades—one big disappointment after another. I can't believe you're really my son. I didn't aim to have a retard."

"Get your lazy-ass butt off that couch and help your mother," he would yell at me if I neglected to help set the table. "You're so stupid and lazy; you'll never be worth anything. Do you think I don't know how lazy you are? Get up. Right now before I teach you what happens to lazy-ass kids."

When I was old enough to realize there were avoidance tactics, I tried to stay out of his path on the days when he seemed edgy and fussy, the days when he prowled the house like a lion looking for a wildebeest to slaughter. My brother and I would play outside until goose bumps formed on our arms and daylight colors turned to shades of gray. Better to play outside and freeze to death than to wander aimlessly inside the house and inadvertently cross our father. Sometimes on those days I would hear him pacing inside, fussing at my mother about a coworker or yelling at her if his favorite socks weren't in the dresser drawer.

For years I thought this was normal family life. It never occurred to me that other children had a different type of father. That is, until I was eight and made friends with Ben. We would ride our bikes to his house after school, and some evenings I would eat dinner with them and absorb the calmness around their table. One night as I pushed soggy canned green beans around my plate, I realized I'd never heard Ben's dad yell in anger. Not once. I'd heard him complain about being tired or about car trouble or about his boss, but Ben's father's frustration never included poisonous barbs aimed at his wife, daughter, or son. My mind was too young to fully process that realization, but somehow I recognized the significance and filed the facts away for future reference.

When I was fourteen, my father was inducted as president of our city's chamber of commerce. The four of us dressed up and drove in our station wagon to the ceremony. My mother, brother, and I had been thoroughly briefed on proper handshake, eye contact, and table manners, undoubtedly to be sure we didn't embarrass my father among his peers. My mother beamed with pride as we walked through the crowd and one after another of my father's colleagues extolled his accomplishments. I don't remember too many details of the evening, except the fact I felt as if everyone was watching to see if I made a mistake. I was nervous beyond belief, knowing I would be reminded of any small error for weeks, possibly months. Fortunately, the evening went smoothly. At the end, as my father was being formally introduced as president, my brother and I listened incredulously as the outgoing president spoke of my father as "a generous and gracious man" and "someone who manages his personal and professional lives with an ever-present spirit of kindness." That was news to us. We had never thought of our father as a kind man. Someone to be respected, pleased, feared—yes, we knew him as that man, but not as someone we would ever describe as kind.

About that time, I began to experience the rumblings of testosterone looking for release. Besides growing four inches in one summer and finding female curves intriguing, I began to feel a fury building inside me. It refused to be ignored, so I tried on my father's temper in ninth grade. I bullied a few smaller guys and threw some equipment around in the locker room after a football game. But within a few months, I found my father's anger didn't fit me. It was hard to lug around and it gave me no satisfaction, so I summarily discarded angry outbursts in favor of logic. I determined I would become the even-tempered, logical thinker who could reason his way out of a problem or smooth talk his way into a party. And I made a commitment to myself that I would never allow my father to relapse in me.

11

I buried myself in my studies through college and law school, which allowed me to talk with my father only when necessary. Our conversations were controlled, measured distributions of bland words. At least on my part, they were. I avoided more subjects than I discussed and I managed to have what most observers would call a good relationship with the man who had haunted my childhood. It seemed to me we had reached a cease-fire. He was satisfied with my progress toward manhood. I was satisfied to speak with him periodically and call him my father.

He died in an auto accident a few months after I married Dayne. My mother was inconsolable. Paul was distant and aloof. I took the news like a man and immediately set about planning his funeral. I approached it with businesslike clarity. I met with the mortuary, the florist, the reverend; provided pictures, a suit to dress him in for burial, his full legal name for all the forms. I was efficient even as my mother cried tears I couldn't fully understand. She was hurting in the most visceral way while I was conducting business. Years before, sometime during my college psychology class, I had put the most painful memories of my father and my childhood into a sealed vault, hoping they would stay buried until I reached senility. I had spent time analyzing my father's effect on me and trying to separate the truth in his words about me from the lies. I had outgrown and outanalyzed his effect on me. I no longer wondered if my father liked me or was proud of me. Sometime during that psych class I stopped wanting his approval. I decided to be true to myself rather than to a man who could never be satisfied.

At the graveside, I stood over my father's casket baking in the August heat and watched his skin flake in snow-like pieces from his lifeless body. I stood there believing I could close the lid on our difficult life together and live at peace with the memories of our good times. After all, we'd had good times: family vacations, dinners together, and Christmas gifts. I believed my days as my father's target were over. I didn't realize I had married his stunt double.

12

4

FOURTH TO NINTH YEAR OF OUR MARRIAGE

I was aware Dayne had family challenges just like I did. I knew that when we moved in together. But her beauty and our mutual chemistry trumped any due diligence I might have done. I enjoyed coming home to a beautiful woman. It helped get me through the rigors of law school. Besides, I loved her and I believed that was the key to the success of any marriage. What I forgot to factor in was the influences of her life before she met me.

Dayne left home at eighteen, one week after she graduated from high school. She and her mother had been on a collision course for years, and when Margie screamed, "Why don't you just leave?" one day, Dayne left. She drove alone from her hometown in Oregon to Southern California and got a job working in a doctor's office. I often wondered how her father could let his only child leave so suddenly—why he didn't step in during the heat of the argument or reason with her while she packed the car, but according to Dayne, her mother ruled the house and her dad didn't interfere. He watched a lot of sports, worked on his cars, and meticulously avoided getting caught between his two women.

"My mother's a mean woman who's always mad about something," Dayne told me early on. "She's vindictive, so my father just checks out. You

13

won't ever have to worry about spending holidays with my parents. I call them a few times a year, but other than that, they're not really a part of my life. They spend their holidays with my uncle and aunt."

I didn't think much of it at the time. I was too busy with law school, and truthfully, it seemed like a benefit to live far from my future in-laws. If we saw them, it would be on our terms. It was the same way I interacted with my parents at the time—I called them, but rarely visited. I saw it as another way Dayne and I were compatible. We could visit family periodically, but they wouldn't really affect our day-to-day lives. Or so I thought. Dayne looked nothing like my father, so I didn't notice the resemblance until it was too late.

We were the parents of two small children when Dayne's harsh words became more frequent and I could no longer make excuses for her verbal attacks. Right around our five-year anniversary, Dayne introduced a new vocabulary to our marital disagreements—words designed to hurt rather than solve: dumb, lazy, selfish. For emphasis she began utilizing the phrase "I'm just telling you this for your own good, Mike." That particular sentence usually preceded a recitation of my faults as perceived by Dayne and her friends.

"I'm telling you this for your own good," she began one day. "Carla's husband, Don, doesn't like you. You're not very much fun at parties, you know, and it's hard to carry on an interesting conversation with you because all you do is talk about yourself. I think I'll just spend time with Carla by myself from now on." I stood there stunned as she walked out of the room. I scoured my memory for any hint of Don's displeasure. We'd been at their house recently for Carla's birthday party, but I'd said only a few words to Don, and those were mostly about his business. I couldn't for the life of me figure out how I'd made a bad impression, so I kept my distance from Don and Carla to keep from embarrassing my wife any further. Making a good impression was important then. I was a young attorney trying to build a practice.

I was neck-deep in building that practice the year MarLea was born. Five years before, when Dayne and I married, I was a fresh graduate working seventy-hour weeks for a large firm. I believed that things at that firm would get better, and perhaps given enough time they would have improved. But I did not have the patience or the spousal support to work those hours indefinitely. So right after our first child was born, my classmate Rob Berger and I decided to open our own firm. Amazingly, we succeeded,

14

thanks largely to our receptionist/office manager, Carol, the wife of a local businessman who knew everyone and promoted our practice shamelessly. In those early years, Carol believed in Passick and Berger even more than Passick and Berger believed in themselves.

Going from seventy hours a week and a guaranteed paycheck to a business of our own with no guarantees was a tough transition, both mentally and emotionally. I put 110 percent into every client, craving referrals and accolades.

Although we had never formally discussed a division of labor along traditional lines, Dayne and I fell into the stereotypical roles. I worked outside the home, and Dayne handled the house and kids. Dayne wanted children as much as I did, but we were both innocently oblivious to the amount of work that arrived with a second child. Dayne had found life at home difficult with one child, and now she was juggling the needs of an active three-year-old and a delicate infant. When I came home, I never knew what I would encounter. Some evenings it was a sobbing wife and crying children. Other times it was a content mother nursing her baby daughter as her son watched a video. Of course, most husbands in this stage of life would say the same thing. Young families are dynamic, and emotions run from highs to lows. I expected some of that. What I didn't expect was Dayne's pillow talk.

"I thought by now we'd be living in Newport," she told me one night as we lay together in bed. "Do you think you'll ever make more money, or will I be stuck in this crappy tract house forever?"

"I thought you liked this house," I responded.

"It's fine...for a starter home," she stated pointedly. "I just didn't think by the time we had our second child we'd still be in something this...oh, I don't know...this small and common."

"Do you want to redecorate?" I asked.

"Are you kidding?" she shot back, as she shifted her body away from me and rolled onto her side, her spine pointing accusations in my direction. "What a waste of money that would be."

"I just thought..."

"You're a selfish idiot," she interrupted, her voice aimed across her shoulder. "You don't even try to understand me or meet my needs. All you think about is yourself and that stupid law office of yours."

I didn't know what to say, so I lay silently in the dark for a while. Because I didn't know how to respond, I reached across to touch her, but she pulled away. Two days later, she was still avoiding my touch, and I found myself avoiding her. I was confused by her level of dissatisfaction with our home. I didn't understand her anger when I suggested redecorating. I decided it was better to stay outside until goose bumps dotted my arms rather than risk irritating her. So I worked late and avoided any direct contact until four days later when she made a nice dinner for all of us and called to say it would be ready at six. I arrived home at five fifty and when I kissed her hello, she didn't turn away. I chose to believe the problem had been solved.

For too long, I was the typical oblivious male. At first I thought Dayne and I had found our comfort zone, which was occasionally interrupted by mood swings or hormones or overwork or frustration. I provided paternal stability by concentrating on my law practice and doing my best to be a caring husband and a good dad. Dayne handled our home life and did her best as a full-time mom. If I didn't microanalyze, it appeared stable, normal, and comfortable. At times it was even amazing, a vast improvement on my own childhood. I remember tossing my kids in the air, helping with baths when I was home, reading bedtime stories to sleepy toddlers. Matt and I would go outside on Sunday mornings when he was just a chubby three-year-old, and we would play chase in the backyard. He was such a happy little boy, so different from the sullen, distant teen he became. On those Sunday mornings, I would run around the backyard with Matt and glance periodically at our bedroom window high above the backyard. Sometimes I could see Dayne's head in the window, her hair glistening in the sun like finely polished obsidian. I loved those mornings—Matt and I running in the damp grass, Dayne with our beautiful baby girl in her arms, and everyone sheltered within our happy home. I loved that feeling of being a family, providing for my wife and kids.

During those years when our children were little, Dayne provided the maternal and social aspects of our lives—taking care of the kids' expanding schedules and keeping us connected to her friends. We managed to carve out a date night once or twice a month that often started with dinner at a well-reviewed restaurant and usually ended with a discussion about the challenges at home. Like many couples, we felt obligated to communicate about our son's upcoming school project or the broken garage door or the leaky faucet, but those conversations left intimacy sitting alone at another table. Our date nights often ended with two tired parents falling into opposite sides of the bed. I assumed it was normal—a stage of life.

"Are you tired?" I asked Dayne one evening after a particularly satisfying dinner at Montage and a surprisingly problem-free conversation.

"Yeah," she answered as she dropped her sweater in the laundry basket and picked up her toothbrush.

I walked over and kissed the back of her neck. She turned and kissed me back. A good sign.

"Look, I'm up for a quickie," she said. "But I have to drive carpool in the morning and I'm really tired." I might have felt momentary disappointment in the flatness of that exchange, but I figured we were pretty normal. A busy couple with kids and responsibilities and stressors. Maybe after the kids were grown we could become a couple of lingering passion again. I hadn't lost hope. After all, we had the skills. We just had to find the time.

We were at a barbecue at Rob and Leanne's house one evening in May. It was the year Matt started Little League. He must have been around six, and he was in the same league as Rob's son. I remember the kids were all playing in the yard, the four of us dads gathered around the grill as Rob cooked burgers. My arms were sunburned from helping at practice that morning. I was feeling very familial and content. It was the picture of suburbia I'd always dreamed of as a child: playful kids, successful dads, content wives all gathered together around good food. Dayne was in the kitchen with the other wives, getting things ready as the meat grilled to perfection.

"Hey, Mike," Rob said in my direction. "Go stick your head in the kitchen and find out if the women want their burgers medium rare or cooked till they beg for mercy." I put down my beer and headed toward the other side of the house.

The air was beginning to cool as I walked around the corner of the house toward the high-pitched voices coming through the kitchen windows. I heard a burst of laughter. Clearly the wives had found the bottle of wine and were enjoying some girl talk. I walked by the window just in time to hear Dayne say, "Well, I could use some excitement in the bedroom. I mean, Mike gets points for effort, but it's pretty clear he never read the

Kama Sutra. Maybe I should just run off with the pool guy. I bet he'd put some spice between my sheets." The women laughed.

I don't remember much of the evening from that point on. I just remember the dry feeling in my mouth and my instant decision to turn around and tell Rob that the women all wanted their burgers well done. I never imagined myself a bedroom genius, but up to that point, I'd always thought I was a few steps above average. I couldn't imagine why Dayne would belittle me to her friends just for a few laughs.

My mind played direct, cross, and redirect with itself most of the night. No man wants to be called a boring or clueless lover. Maybe I'd misunderstood the conversation. Maybe I took something out of context.

I thought about asking Dayne for clarification after we left that night and decided it would only result in deeper wounds. No amount of mental contortions ever led me to picture an outcome better than, "Well, it's true. You're a disappointment in the bedroom." So I decided to avoid hearing those words actually spoken.

It was the first time in my life I wished I'd taken my brother's route. Instead of turning to logic for his solace, he'd closed off his emotional spigot and distanced himself from our family of origin as soon as he turned eighteen. He had chosen a college far from home. Within days of his high school graduation, he'd permanently moved a full continent away, never to return. I realized that night my brother may never feel close to anyone. He may be emotionally stunted for the rest of his life. But he had successfully avoided the searing pain I kept experiencing. The feeling that over and over, I kept putting my beating heart in the hands of someone I thought loved me, and over and over I kept watching her laugh as she dropped it into a frying pan.

For years after the barbecue at Rob and Leanne's house, thoughts I had sublimated since childhood began working their way out of my subconscious like tapeworms. I began to wonder if my father had been correct. Maybe I was the problem. Maybe it was up to me to change and become a man my wife could love and respect—the man who kept her passion alive. I began reading books and listening to self-help tapes, trying to learn how to fully meet the needs of my wife. I decided I would devote myself to making Dayne happy. I would work harder, become a better lover, provide a more beautiful home, help with the kids more, be sure she drove an upscale car, and take her on lavish vacations. Maybe that way I could finally earn her unconditional love.

5

NINTH YEAR OF OUR MARRIAGE

I don't know what I expected would happen when I decided to work harder, become a better husband, provide more. I just know all that effort did nothing to cement feelings of unconditional love inside me, and it did little to improve Dayne's moods. If I had to use one word to describe the first nine years of my marriage to Dayne, that word would be *perplexing*.

Little by little, almost as imperceptibly as the maturing of the landscape at our beautiful new home and the growth of our children, I watched my wife become more and more dissatisfied with the life I provided.

Coming home at night became a game of spinning the roulette wheel. One night I would walk in to contentment and another night I would walk in on chaos. I'm sure that sounds typical for any household with small children. I wasn't ignorant of the challenges Dayne faced as she raised our kids and managed our household. She'd given up her career as a medical office manager to stay home, and I knew she both loved and resented that choice. But it had been her choice, so I didn't quite understand why the challenges at home seemed to destroy her happiness and why the roulette wheel kept stopping at anger. I especially didn't understand why the anger kept homing in on me. I was consistently the target.

21

I kept looking for hints in the faces of other domesticated men: the fathers holding purses and infants outside restroom doors, the men driving minivans through the Target parking lot on weekends. Some had the same confused look I wore, but most simply looked resigned or tired. I took comfort in the playful couples I'd occasionally see loading groceries into the back of a car together or walking on either side of a hand-holding toddler. "See," I would say to myself, "everyone has good days and bad days. Every guy takes his turn with confusion, exhaustion, and then happiness and fun. It's the circle of life for adult males. It's normal."

Then I would walk into Hurricane Dayne on one of her especially bad days. Those were the most confusing of all, not because of her anger, but because I couldn't tell what I'd done wrong. The air would be thick with tension and the children would be hunkered down in front of the TV or playing quietly in another room. I would walk through the door unaware—there were no hints, no clues to alert me, no sign on the door that said "Bad day, enter at your own risk." So like any unsuspecting prey, I would walk right into the trap and not realize I was caught until the steel door swung shut.

It might start as innocently as setting my laptop on the table when I walked through the door. I remember one particular evening.

"Just throw it anywhere," Dayne said.

"What?"

"How hard would it be to walk five more feet and put it in the study?"

"I can do that if you want."

"Sure, make me the bad guy," Dayne said.

"What?"

"You're a slob so you make me the bad guy because I want to keep this house clean. I work all day to keep the kids from trashing the few nice things we have, and you don't care where you throw your stuff."

"Dayne, I wasn't trying to..."

"Give me a break, Mike. You never pick up anything. You think I'm your maid. Well, I'm not. I'm your wife and if you were any husband at all you'd treat me like you loved me and not like hired help."

By then I was so confused I didn't have a clue what to do. I tried to think if I'd left a towel on the floor that morning, or if I'd missed throwing my dirty socks into the hamper last night. I was sure the towel was hung up and the socks were in the hamper. So l just stood there looking at her, which infuriated her more.

"Sure, just stand there."

"What do you want me to do, Dayne?"

"Pick up your damn stuff. Quit treating me like your Playboy Bunny maid. You're so stinkin' selfish, and I'm sick of it. I'm sick of it all. I'm especially sick of you."

I lifted my laptop case off the table, the same table where I'd left it many times before with no outburst, and began walking toward the study. Dayne kept working in the kitchen. I stayed in the study until she called us all to dinner. Then I sat quietly in my designated place, hoping to avoid an encore. There are some things worth fighting over. In my mind, a laptop on a table didn't deserve more than one heated exchange, so I kept a low profile even after we went to bed.

If you put me in a room with four FBI agents, three spotlights, and a gun pointed at my head right now and told me to logically explain that confrontation or die, I couldn't do it. I still don't understand what happened on those days—the days of her unexpected anger. I would spend hours trying to figure out if I'd missed an anniversary, neglected a child's event, or inadvertently overlooked a promised midday phone call. But I could never figure it out. I remained in a state of cyclical confusion, followed by brief periods of bliss. Every once in a while, I'd come home to an aroused wife. She would greet me at the door with kisses and whispers that the kids were gone to friends' homes. She would entice me upstairs with her mischievous walk and her beautiful pout, and we would make love with the daylight still shining through the windows.

But I could never predict whether I would be greeted with anger or passion.

They say rats lose their minds when life is unpredictable. When the rats press the same lever and one day pellets drop and another day they receive a shock, researchers say it drives the rats crazy. I believe it. I don't know if I was actually going crazy. But I know I began to doubt myself. I began to doubt if I was the man I had always believed myself to be—a man of kindness, a man of strength, a man who was a good husband and father. I began to wonder who I really was. Maybe I was a slob, maybe I was a mediocre husband, maybe I was inferior stock. Maybe my father had been right all along—I would never be worthy of love and acceptance. Maybe I deserved the anger.

During those times, work was my therapy. There was always plenty of work to do. Rob and I were fortunate to have a growing clientele with increasing needs for contract law. Somehow it felt better to retreat into my study and the richness of Tchaikovsky or drive to my office to face a looming deadline than to yell back at my wife. I'd heard enough yelling as a child, and I didn't want to subject my children to the same cacophony. When I was young, the sound of my parents at war had burned my ears and dried my mouth to the point I could barely swallow. It was searing pain that took away all vestiges of my security. There were times I felt my father's anger was capable of incinerating our home. My mother rarely fought back, but when she did, I cowered in my room and cried into my pillow. No boy should feel that helpless when his mother is being destroyed one word at a time. But I did...I felt completely helpless as a child. And I was determined my children would never feel those eviscerating emotions.

So instead of fighting back, yelling, or bullying, I retreated into work. At work I was strong, capable, in control of the outcome. I was the man I wanted to be at work. At home I wasn't sure who I was or what was happening. I was perpetually perplexed.

6

EARLY YEARS OF MY LAW PRACTICE

Rob and I are perfect business partners. We became friends our second year of law school when our individual desire to win the competition against every other classmate in the room was replaced by a realization we had to pass the bar. A few of us formed a study group, and Rob and I became friends. We studied hard and when the information became too thick to absorb, we'd take his boat and head to the lake for a couple of hours of waterskiing. Sometimes it was cool, so we'd take wetsuits. Most of the time it was sunny—just the vitamin D break we needed after living in the tombs of legal jargon. Rob and I both relished this time with our women. Dayne was working as an office manager for Dr. Gartiner, who practiced internal medicine near the university. She was always off by five thirty and ready to jump into her bikini. She would grab burgers and fries on her way home, and we'd have the boat hooked up to his black pickup, ready to leave by the time she arrived. Rob had just begun dating Leanne that year. A diminutive redhead with ridiculous proportions, Leanne wore bikini tops that defied physics. I never figured out how that amount of fabric could hold in that amount of womanhood, but those bikini tops never failed her. Men couldn't help but look, and every time another man looked at Leanne, Rob just smiled. He didn't have a jealous bone in his body, and he knew Leanne was crazy about him. She told him later she knew from the first date that he was her man, but she was an old-fashioned girl who didn't fool around and didn't open her heart too freely. They married six months after their first date, and Leanne was pregnant within months. By graduation, Dayne and I had been living together for a while and were talking about marriage. Rob and Leanne were already burping their first child.

Both Rob and I thought large multiname firms were the goal after graduation. He needed steady money to support his growing family. I needed the prestige to prove something to myself. We were both chosen by good firms and went our separate ways, but neither of us found the professional life we wanted in those large buildings and small cubicles. We toiled away on other attorneys' cases and came home night after night with no sense of real accomplishment. For two competitive men, it was torture. I thought I'd stick it out until Rob and I ran into each other at a mutual friend's party in April. One phone call, one dinner with the wives—Dayne and I were parents by then—and we decided to open our own firm. We specialized in contract law, and when a few businessmen of stature in the community used our firm and liked the results, our clientele grew rapidly. Between Carol's connections and the referrals during that first year, we actually started to exhale all that pent-up fear of failure. It was another step in my healing, I thought, because I'd proved my father wrong. I was not going to fail in life. I had the intelligence to make good choices and reap the success. I was going to have a great life.

Rob's sense of humor and a natural optimism helped cement our partnership. He's a born optimist, although you have to know him well to see it because he's also naturally quiet, thoughtful, and analytical. He wasn't the first guy anyone noticed in law school because he's average looking and average height with average brown hair and average clothing choices. But when Rob spoke, you rarely forgot him or his words. He was voted president of our graduating class. One professor said Rob was the first "shy president" a senior class had ever elected. Most of us ignored the comment because Rob is definitely not shy. His thoughts are just too interesting and too rich to throw around indiscriminately.

Rob is a bit of a tease too. Early on in our practice, he started pinning cartoons above the copy machine. Usually it was a *Far Side* cartoon that made us all laugh, but different things started appearing on the wall from time to time—a tattered and faded playbill from *Hair* with an arrow pointing to one woman and the words "Carol, is that you?" or a memo advising me that the Darth Vader masks I'd ordered were due to arrive in five days. His sense of humor was bizarre but playful.

"You better learn to golf soon," Rob teased as I walked by his office during our first year together. "'Cause I'm going to be making deals on the ninth hole with all the executives in this town."

"Oh really?" I said.

"Yup."

"You taking lessons?"

"Sure am," Rob said.

He didn't need to say another word. We were both twelve-handicap golfers within two years. Rob had gone to a few chamber of commerce meetings, heard all the golf talk in the halls, and decided it was in our best interest to become golfers. I liked the way he analyzed situations, made decisions, and acted on them. I also liked the way he made it obvious I needed to change without ever telling me what to do. He was a good partner then, and it's only gotten better through the years. We have an ability to communicate effectively without too many words, and an ability to care for each other without too much baggage. Truthfully, Rob is my brother. We just don't happen to have the same parents. Probably a good thing.

I've heard it said a three-legged stool is a very stable design, because the pressure points are well spread out and each leg must carry its share of the weight. After watching our law practice during those first couple of years, I was a believer. Rob, Carol, and I were like three legs of a well-designed stool. Carol handled the phones, the computer, the finances, and made every client feel adored. She was a phenomenal receptionist, so we quickly promoted her to office manager and gave her a wide swath of authority.

I remember the early years well. I'd walk in around eight fifteen. Carol would be sitting at her desk, her short blond hair tucked behind her ears as she concentrated on her work. She always wore large earrings with flower or agate designs that perfectly matched her clothing. I don't remember much about her clothing choices because they were always appropriate, so I had no reason to take note. In fact, that's what I remember most about Carol in those early years. She was always appropriate and capable. She was the stability Rob and I leaned on as we navigated self-employment. Rob and I were hardly thirty when we opened our practice. Carol was already facing an empty nest and planning all the trips she and her husband, J. C., would take when he retired. Truthfully, she was probably a mother figure in our office. But at the time it didn't seem as if she mothered the clients or us. It just seemed comfortable and nice to have her around. Like a warm fire spilling light and heat throughout the reception area, Carol just made you want to be near her, because you knew good things were going to happen as long as she was around.

"You think we're being good employers?" Rob asked one day as I walked past his open office door. We were both working late so we could skip out and golf the next afternoon.

I stopped walking and stuck my head in his doorway.

"You're asking?"

"Yeah," Rob said, "just asking."

"Why?"

"I'm not sure," he said. "I guess because I'm starting to think of Carol more like a partner in this practice."

"Yeah, it does feel that way a little," I agreed.

"So is that how we're supposed to treat an employee?"

"Got me," I said quickly. "I've never done this before. But I think she's a great person, and she's doing a bang-up job for us."

"She really is," Rob said confidently.

I nodded and then headed back toward my office. I never gave it another thought until years later. At the time, Rob and I were young, buried in work, and figuring things out as we went along. We couldn't predict the future so chose to believe it would be perpetually good. I read a quote the other day attributed to Albert Schweitzer. He said, "An optimist is a person who sees a green light everywhere, while a pessimist sees only the red stoplight...A truly wise person is colorblind." I should have read that a long time ago. It might have saved me a lot of pain at home and at the office. Then again, who's to say it would have made any difference. Rob and I were both born looking for green lights.

28

7

NINTH AND TENTH YEARS OF OUR MARRIAGE

I tried to ignore the pain in my marriage for a while, but it's hard to ignore gangrene. Verbal attacks on your personhood, the core of who you are, are like that. They start as a small red line running up the leg of your marriage, a warning that there's poison inside. And if you ignore them, the marriage becomes ill, and then it starts to die one appendage at a time.

I remember the first time I thought our marriage might have a serious flaw. I was at a legal conference in Seattle, and the topic "Psychological Terms from a Legal Perspective" looked like an interesting breakout session. The speaker threw around many terms, and verbal abuse would have gotten buried in the mix except I'd already come to the conclusion I was a verbally abused child. This day, for whatever reason, I thought for just a second that maybe Dayne fit the pattern too. That was the moment my internal debate began. I was a happily married man with two small children. I was dealing with the same challenges every marriage faced. If you would have asked my mother, she would have told you the same thing. I could just imagine the conversation.

29

"Mom, do you think Dad was a verbally abusive husband?"

"Oh, honey, of course not. Where'd you even hear that term? Your dad was a good man. He loved us."

"But, Mom, he used to berate you—say horrible, demeaning things to Paul and me and especially to you."

"Well, sure, son. Everyone says things sometimes—things they probably shouldn't say. But we just forgive them and go on. Your dad was human just like everyone else. I forgave him and went on."

So I buried the idea that Dayne might fit the pattern of verbal abuse deep in my subconscious and had no cause to resurrect it. It stayed safely entombed for many years. Whenever Dayne and I would argue, I found other terms to contextualize the problem: PMS, overwork, Mars/Venus. Those satisfied me through the hours or days of conflict.

Of course, I told myself. All women call their husbands lazy, inconsiderate, and selfish. These are some of the most used words in the English language when spouses fight. That's what I'd tell myself.

"Mike, are you ever going to get me a decent car?" Dayne asked one rainy day as she carried a bag of groceries in from the garage. The kids were playing upstairs, and the smell of chili filled the kitchen. I'd arrived home just in time to help unload the cargo.

"What?" I asked, my hands full of laundry detergent and paper towels. "Is something wrong with your car?"

"This car drives me crazy. I'm sick of problems all the time."

Dayne had been forced to call AAA two days before when she discovered a flat tire at the grocery store. I was in Boston, boarding a plane to come home after a legal conference. I knew waiting for a tow truck would be challenging with kids, but she'd handled it. I had thought my kisses and words of gratitude when I walked in the door had ended the story, but suddenly, we were talking about it again.

"Another car wouldn't prevent flat tires."

"It's not the only thing wrong with the car."

"What else is wrong?"

"It's old, Mike." Her voice rose slightly. "It's five years old and it's a minivan and it's been used a lot and it doesn't run like a new car anymore. Get it?"

30

"Yeah," I replied, frustration starting to edge into my voice. "I know it's not new, but it still runs well."

"No, it doesn't."

"Then what's wrong? Tell me what the problem is, and we'll get it fixed."

Dayne stopped putting groceries away and looked directly at me. She stood there silently for a moment, narrowed her eyes, shook her head slightly, and said, "You can really tell who's loved in this neighborhood. Take a look around and notice the women with the big rocks and the nice cars. Then look in our garage. It'll tell you everything you need to know."

Nothing in law school prepared me for arguments like this. I searched quickly for the logical steps between a flat tire and being loved, but I couldn't find them. So I just stood there looking at her. Looking for something I never ever found in all the years we were married—how to make sense of her accusations and how to tell if they were true.

"Sure, just stand there like a dumbass," Dayne said, her face filled with anger.

"What do you want me to say?" I responded.

"You're the genius lawyer," she shot back. "You figure something out."

Dayne walked loudly into the utility room and began slamming cabinet doors. I stood there, my hands heavy on the countertop, deciding what to do. If I left, I could be accused of not caring. If I stayed, the argument would undoubtedly escalate. There was no way out. I sat in the nearest chair to await the execution that never came. Finally I walked into my study and put on Tchaikovsky's Piano Concerto in C major. The slow, gentle pace of this concerto can always soothe me. I sat quietly in my chair picturing days on the lake skiing behind Rob's boat. I wanted to believe that beautiful, sexy Dayne who sat in Rob's boat soaking up the sunshine in her blue-and-gold-striped bikini wasn't the same woman who'd just accused me of not loving her enough. I searched my mind for what might have caused this metamorphosis, and I settled on the culprit. It had to be my long hours at work combined with something that had happened in her day. She was tired. I worked too much. But I couldn't for the life of me figure out a way to stop working those hours. Circular head games—enough to make you really crazy. I probably should have put on Red Hot Chili Peppers' "Can't

31

Stop." It would have been more appropriate to my mood. But instead I just sat quietly trying to calm myself so I could go crawl into bed with Dayne and pretend nothing had happened. It was the best way to keep the peace at home so I could keep the pieces together at work.

I knew in my heart something was terribly wrong. But it was unfixable. Even if you diagnose the disease, you can't always find a cure. Somewhere during our tenth and eleventh anniversaries, I began to see the line of gangrene running up the leg of our marriage. Limping and pain had begun to feel like a normal gait to us. Someday, I suspected we would have to address the cause and dig it out before the entire marriage died. But we were both too tired and too busy to do it. There was too much work at my office, and too many activities that required Dayne to carpool. We were both just too busy to concentrate on a single red line.

8

JANUARY, TWELFTH YEAR OF OUR MARRIAGE

Carol's husband died suddenly and unexpectedly on a brisk January morning three weeks after Christmas. He called her at the office about 10:00 a.m. and told her he was staying home because he didn't feel well. She found his lifeless body in the recliner when she got home that evening. Her first call was 911. I got the second frantic phone call as Dayne, Matt, MarLea, and I sat eating dinner together.

I left immediately and spent the next three days helping Carol call her two grown kids and other relatives, plan the funeral, and figure out how to face widowhood. Rob handled the office, I handled Carol. Both were daunting tasks.

I'm not sure what I expected to find when I entered Carol's house after her initial call. She'd always been so capable and competent at the office, so I wasn't fully prepared to see her, hands clasped in a bone-breaking grip and face in total shock as the coroner loaded J. C.'s body into his van. The sheriff's deputy left as soon as I arrived, and suddenly it was just Carol and me huddled at her table, listening to the dial tone as we began to call her children. Something was missing in this house, something important. Life. I sat at the kitchen table beside her as she cried through the calls to her son and daughter. Exhausted

33

after those calls, her face ashen and her eyes swollen from crying, Carol simply wrote down a few more names, opened the contact list on her computer, and asked me to finish notifying her relatives and friends. I watched as Carol walked into the family room, sat in J. C.'s still-warm recliner, and stared out the window. She wasn't crying. She just sat in the last place she had seen J. C.'s body before it was loaded into the coroner's van.

The first few calls went as expected. Carol's sister in Missouri cried out when she heard the news. She and her husband would catch a plane as soon as possible. Thank you for calling. Good-bye. J. C.'s brother had just had hip surgery and couldn't travel, but he wanted to know the details and made me promise I would call him each day to provide updates. Next were the nieces and nephews. Carol requested I call her niece Brooke first.

"She's a very capable woman," Carol said. "She'll know what to do. She'll help you. I can't think right now."

I dialed the number.

"Hi, this is Brooke Westin. Please leave a message and I'll return your call at my earliest convenience."

"Brooke, my name is Mike Passick. Your aunt Carol works at my office, and I have some sad news about your uncle. Please call me back at this number. Thank you."

Seven calls and forty minutes later, Brooke returned my call.

"Mike, this is Brooke. What happened?" She spoke quickly and her voice was filled with concern.

"Thanks for calling me back. I'm so sorry, Brooke. Your uncle passed away this afternoon."

"Oh no." Brooke's voice quavered. She sighed heavily. "No."

"I'm so sorry" was all I could say.

Like all the others, she was gracious but stricken and fighting tears. "When did he die?"

"Sometime this afternoon—your aunt found him in his recliner when she got home from work."

The phone was silent for a few seconds before Brooke spoke again.

"Is Aunt Carol all right?"

"She's in shock. Once she called her kids, she hasn't moved from the chair."

"Oh."

More silence.

"I'll catch a flight out as soon as I can, probably this evening," Brooke said suddenly, firmly. "Just let Aunt Carol know I'll be there as quickly as I can."

"I'll tell her."

"Thank you for calling. I just can't believe this."

I made a few more calls after Brooke said good-bye. Carol's neighbors and church friends. People began arriving within minutes. I answered the door, offered beverages, and began thinking about ways to accommodate all the relatives who would be arriving within a day. Brooke called back a few minutes later.

"Mike, I'm sorry to bother you."

"No problem."

"I'm sure Carol's kids and grandkids will be staying with her, so can you recommend a hotel nearby? I could take my chances online, but it seems wiser to take your recommendation. My parents and I will be flying out first thing tomorrow morning. Our flights arrive within thirty minutes of each other, so I'll rent a car, get us all settled into the hotel, and then come over to help."

I recommended a hotel near Carol's house and instantly realized that Brooke's arrival would be a huge help. Carol was right. This niece was organized and capable. She was already thinking two steps ahead.

I stayed at Carol's house until after midnight. The last of Carol's neighbors left, and her friend Mary Lou offered to spend the night with her, so I headed home and crawled into bed just after one. Dayne curled up next to me and kissed me lightly on the shoulder before she drifted back to sleep. I stayed awake for nearly an hour, thinking about how quickly and unexpectedly life can end, how grateful I was for Dayne's warm body next to mine, and how sad I was that Carol would never again feel J. C. lying next to her.

The next morning I woke up at five thirty, wide awake. It was as if my brain was ordering my body to get up and get moving...things to do. I moved quietly around the room in the dark, gathering clothes so I could shower in the guest bathroom. I was out the door by six fifteen to handle things at the office before I headed to Carol's house. About the time Rob arrived I was leaving, so I gave him the quick update and we decided to continue the divide-and-conquer tactics. He'd oversee the office, and I'd head to Carol's house to do whatever I could.

Brooke and her parents arrived just before noon. I was near the front door when they arrived, so I was the first to greet them. Brooke's mother, Carol's only sister, was a mirror image of Carol. They might have been twins except for the difference in hair color and height. Her husband, a large man in both height and weight, greeted me with a warm handshake.

"Thank you for calling us, son," he said, as if I were a member of his immediate family. "This is such a shock. We came right away."

I nodded. Behind him, I noticed a brunette about my age pulling a computer case from the trunk of the car. Even from a distance, she threw off concentric rings of confidence that struck me in waves. It was hard to take my eyes off her. Her movements were athletic, strong, determined. She was petite yet she slammed the trunk lid with a firm hand and walked up the sidewalk toward her father and me.

"Hi, I'm Brooke," she said as her father released my hand and headed toward the living room.

"I'm Mike," I said, aware of her businesslike handshake and the small size of her hand. Dayne's hands were elegantly long and fragile. This hand was small yet strong.

"Let me hug Aunt Carol," Brooke said. "Then I'll be right back to help."

For the next two days, Brooke and I worked together to meet the constant deadlines of an impending funeral. I called Dayne once or twice during the day to be sure everything at home was under control. She assured me everything was fine. It was a relief to know the house was handled and the office was under Rob's care. It allowed me to focus on helping Carol. She seemed to have many friends and relatives to share her grief and sit beside her, but few besides Brooke seemed able or willing to handle all the looming details. Carol's son and daughter were in shock, alternating between disbelief and gut-wrenching sorrow, so they made the big decisions and left all the small details to Brooke, who adeptly organized everything. Carol's house was bursting at the seams with friends and relatives. I answered the phone and stayed near the door to greet guests and receive the warm casseroles and thickly frosted desserts neighbors brought. Brooke established a system in the kitchen that provided a well-stocked buffet when anyone needed food. No one went hungry. As the day progressed, relatives found a spot to sit or a place to help. Some sat at the table and searched through pictures for the photo tribute; others ordered the flowers and helped deliver J. C.'s clothes to the mortuary. I began writing a life sketch as Brooke canvassed family members for special memories. Together we edited and rewrote until the document finally felt like a fitting tribute to J. C.

"Thank you for all your help, Mike," Brooke said as I closed my laptop at ten thirty and stood to leave. "I couldn't have done it without you."

"Glad to help," I said.

"You're a lifesaver for me," she said. I noticed for the first time that her eyes were blue and the corners of her mouth turned up slightly, even when she was sad. "Will you come just a bit early tomorrow...maybe an hour before the funeral starts?"

"Sure," I said.

"I want to be sure the funeral home has everything they need, and it will take a little effort to help my parents get there and settled on time."

"No problem," I said, putting my laptop into its case. "I'll see you about two thirty tomorrow."

I drove home in silence that night. There wasn't any music that sounded appealing, and I didn't want to hear anyone's radio opinion. I was bone tired.

The next day Dayne went to the funeral with me. She looked elegant in her dark dress and the diamond earrings I'd given her for her thirtieth birthday. Brooke asked the two of us if we would stand near the guestbook to be sure everyone signed it, so we greeted guests, helped people find the restrooms, and took our seats just before the service started. I held Dayne's hand through the entire service and watched as Brooke finally cried after days of delaying her grief in order to help others.

As we stood to one side after the service, Dayne and I still holding hands and waiting until most of the guests had said their good-byes, I leaned over to whisper in my wife's ear.

"Thank you for being here with me."

"I wouldn't be anywhere else," Dayne said.

37

We spent an hour or so at Carol's house afterward, saying our good-byes to the family and hugging Carol one last time.

"Thank you so much for sharing your husband with our family during this difficult time," Carol said to Dayne as we were leaving. "I know you gave up a lot of family time, and I'm grateful."

Dayne nodded and hugged her. I felt so proud of my wife. Her ability to remain composed and elegant in difficult situations was one of the things I loved most about her.

"Thanks for all your help, Mike," Brooke said as she walked us to the door. "I'm so incredibly grateful for everything you did."

"I'm glad I could help," I said. The truth was, Brooke and I had contributed a team effort. She was being gracious. I wanted to say how amazed I was by her abilities and her contributions, but Dayne spoke first.

"It was nice to meet you, Brooke," Dayne said. "I know Carol is grateful you're here."

"Nice to meet you too," Brooke replied. "I'm glad I was able to come and help.

"Please keep an eye on my aunt," Brooke said in our direction, almost as an afterthought. "I'm concerned she'll have a very hard time after her kids leave."

"We will," Dayne said.

As we drove home, I was hit with a level of exhaustion that rivaled law school exams. The emotional drain and sadness hit me hard. I came home, undressed, lay down on the bed, and felt as if I'd gone nine rounds with a very good boxer. My brain hurt and my heart was breaking for Carol and her family. I'd barely seen my family in days. Dayne had handled the house, the kids, everything. Now she came and lay beside me in another amazing supportive gesture.

"Are you all right?" she asked tenderly. "I've been worried about you."

"I don't know." It was the only answer I had.

We lay there together for what seemed like an hour, her arm protectively across my chest and her breath grazing my shoulder.

"Thank you for being so supportive," I said after a long silence. "It's been so hard on Carol. I hope you never have to go through that."

Dayne didn't say anything. She just lay there quietly and stroked the side of my arm.

"Do you think she'll keep working?" she asked after another long silence.

"Probably," I answered. "J. C. had some life insurance, but I doubt it's enough to carry her. She's only in her fifties."

"Maybe she'll sell J. C.'s part of the business," Dayne said.

"Maybe, but that'll take a while, unless his partner buys it."

We lay there in silence again, listening for the sounds of the kids' video game. The babysitter had left, and a video game had stepped in to fill the void.

"Don't ever leave me like that," Dayne said suddenly. I felt a tear drop from her face onto my shoulder. "I don't know what I'd do if you ever..."

"Baby," I said, before she finished the thought, "I won't ever leave you. I'm going to live to a ripe old age."

"Promise me," she said as she kissed me.

"I promise."

All the worries I'd had about our marriage, about the increasing venom in her outbursts, about her not-so-subtle hints that I was inadequate, all those worries vanished in a new wave of appreciation and love. Surely our marriage was good, our relationship sound. If we could just bottle this moment and apportion it out over our lifetimes, we would smooth out the ups and downs and enjoy a lifetime of happiness together. I just had to figure out what I could do to capture this moment and never let go.

9

FEBRUARY, TWELFTH YEAR OF OUR MARRIAGE

Carol's niece Brooke called me four weeks after the funeral. It was a brief conversation, but I enjoyed hearing her voice again. She began by thanking me for all my kindness to the family during her uncle's funeral. We talked briefly about Carol and our mutual admiration of her as a person and our concerns for her as a new widow. Brooke had one simple question about California contract law as it related to a possible business deal. She thanked me for my time, and I assured her there was no charge. It was a simple, pleasant call.

I didn't think of it again until a couple of days later when she casually strolled through my thoughts. I'll admit I found Brooke attractive, sensual. We worked well together, and I appreciated her organizational skills in the middle of a family crisis. Fortunately all the positive things I thought about Brooke were irrelevant; she lived four states away and I was a married man with two kids. Besides, what kind of jerk has sexual thoughts about a woman he met at a funeral?

It was a busy time at work, and I didn't think about Brooke again for a while. Carol was still recovering from the shock of J. C.'s death, so Rob and I were doing a lot of our own paperwork. Rob and I had made a pledge to ourselves that we'd keep Carol's job open for her until she told us otherwise. We knew it could be many months before she was able to make that decision. In the meantime, we were busy doing legal, office management, and clerical work.

It seemed the more I worked, the more irritated and demanding Dayne became. She was never one to bring me my slippers as I walked through the door, but now when I walked in the house, often as late as nine or ten at night, she would glance my way with disdain. I usually just went upstairs and fell into bed, giving her a perfunctory kiss as I walked to our bedroom.

"You forgot Matt's game again," she threw at me one night as I struggled to stay awake and listen. "You think I don't notice you have time to run to Carol's side for days when she needs you but can't manage to spend a couple hours watching your own son's football game." It was true. I'd put everything aside to help Carol, and yet I'd look up in the middle of an afternoon call and realize I'd completely missed the first half of Matt's game, and even if I left at that moment, I'd arrive midway through the last quarter. I always felt bad. I would sometimes leave Matt a message that said something like, "Hey, buddy, sorry I missed your game. Hope you did great. See you tonight," and then plow into the piles that grew like freshly spewed lava all over my desk.

One late afternoon, when I was feeling particularly exhausted and wanted to talk to anyone but Dayne, I walked into Rob's office and sat down. He looked up in curiosity from the case he'd been studying.

"Need something?" he asked.

"Just a break," I replied. I sat there in silence for a couple of minutes.

"You think we should hire a temp?" I asked Rob.

"Maybe," he said, eyes still scanning a page. "It could be a while before Carol comes back."

"If she ever does."

"You think she'll quit?"

"I don't know." I sighed. "She might be able to if she sells J. C.'s half of the company. And she did have some life insurance."

"Yeah," Rob said. His eyes went back to the work for a moment, and then he looked at me and said, "Maybe we should hire someone temporarily just to take the pressure off us and off her."

42

"I think it's a good idea," I said. "The clerical stuff is getting ahead of me, and I need to spend more time at home."

"Problems?" Rob asked.

"Just the standard stuff. I need to show up to Matt's games more consistently, and Dayne feels a little neglected."

Rob nodded.

"So you want me to call an agency?" I asked.

"Sure."

And that's how Megan became our temporary receptionist, the person who answered our calls, typed our letters, and provided Dayne with a fresh round of verbal bullets to shoot my direction.

10

APRIL, TWELFTH YEAR OF OUR MARRIAGE

Megan was fresh out of school with a corporate communications major and a résumé short on experience. She was a quick typist and had a nice phone voice, so she got a job with a temp agency so she could afford to travel to places like Bali and Prague. Travel was her inspiration, the reason she got up in the morning and came to work. She showed up on time, dressed professionally, and took care of the mundane so we could concentrate on our clients. Rob and I never had a single reason to complain about her work during the time she worked for us. Not so my wife. Dayne hated her for reasons I still don't understand. The only hint I had were a few comments Dayne made during that time.

"Carol must hate having a little slut sitting at her desk."

"I can't believe you and Rob would hire a child to do Carol's job."

"That Megan idiot you hired put me on hold for over three minutes today. Obviously, she had no idea I was your wife!"

Dayne's defense of Carol baffled me. Although Dayne had supportively attended J. C.'s funeral, she had never considered Carol or J. C. close friends of hers. Now, to hear her trash-talk about Megan, Carol was a saint

45

and a dear friend worth protecting. To say I was surprised would be an understatement.

I assumed it was just part of being a guy. Judging from the fraternity talk in college, we guys were routinely blindsided or confused by women, and I had no reason to think it wouldn't continue into family life. After all, men are from Mars. So I handled the Megan situation the same way I always handled the confusing situations I kept encountering with Dayne. I kept my head down and tried to keep the peace.

If I noticed tension building on a Sunday afternoon, I'd offer to watch the kids while she went out for a while. It was an offer she never refused, and she usually came back with a kiss for me. I'm no fool—I respond well to positive reinforcement. I knew Dayne didn't particularly enjoy hanging out with some of my friends, so I found convenient excuses to decline their invitations and was usually rewarded with peace at home. I became adept at anticipating conflict and deft at maneuvering myself into the place of a human shield. If swords were drawn or grenades thrown, I was usually the one who absorbed the impact, and most times it was just a flesh wound. I considered myself a strong man, a warrior, a provider. I could ignore flesh wounds. I could handle the pain. But Dayne still seemed discontented. There was a look of dissatisfaction in her eyes that simply never went away no matter how I tried to protect her from anything that might upset her.

11

JUNE, TWELFTH YEAR OF OUR MARRIAGE

I got an unexpected phone call from Brooke in June.

"I'm sorry to bother you," she began apologetically. "I'm in town pursuing that business opportunity and wondered if you have a minute to share your opinion about it either today or tomorrow."

"Where are you now?" I asked. My ten-thirty client had just rescheduled as I was heading back to the office, and frankly I was in no hurry to rush back.

"I just arrived at Long Beach. I'm still waiting for my luggage; then I'm taking a cab to the hotel."

"How about if I pick you up and we can talk over lunch?" I offered. "I'm on my way back to the office, and I'm going right by the airport. I can drop you off at your hotel. It'll save you cab fare."

"That would be great," Brooke said. "Are you sure it's convenient on such short notice?"

"It's actually perfect timing. I'll be there in about fifteen minutes."

Brooke was dressed impeccably in light silk shirt and black pants. Even if I wasn't looking for her, I would have noticed her standing at the curb.

47

Her hair was a little lighter than I remembered. Her figure was better than I remembered.

"This is so sweet of you," Brooke said as I loaded her bag into the trunk. "You didn't have to go out of your way, but I'm grateful."

"It's no problem, really," I said. "Carol's done so much for Rob and me. She basically grew our business single-handedly. I'm glad to do anything I can to help her or her family."

Brooke smiled. "My aunt Carol is amazing, isn't she?" Brooke's voice had a lingering sadness that seemed at odds with her smile.

We talked for a few minutes about Carol and the difficult task of grieving. I'd called Carol a few times to see how she was doing, but I didn't honestly know how she was surviving this first year alone. Brooke assured me Carol was breathing through the fingers of grief that kept grabbing at her throat.

"She's got incredible support from her kids and from family and friends," Brooke said, her voice filled with care and compassion. "It's helping her move from simple survival to a place where she can begin to enjoy life again."

I liked the way Brooke had phrased that: a life moving from survival to enjoyment.

We had a nice lunch and I answered a few more questions about the business opportunity. By the time I dropped her off at the hotel, we were laughing about California drivers and freeways.

"Thanks so much," she said as the doorman opened her car door. She placed a hand gently on the sleeve of my shirt. "I can't thank you enough for your wise counsel. I just don't know all the legal considerations in California and don't want to fall into a hole."

"Glad to help," I said, smiling. "Anytime you need counsel, just call."

"I will," she said, and then she was gone. I was stunned to realize I wished she wasn't. "Why?" I asked myself. Then I knew. It felt so good to be appreciated by a woman, to feel relaxed and valued by her, even if it was only for ninety minutes.

12

OCTOBER, OUR THIRTEENTH ANNIVERSARY

"Are you glad you married me?" Dayne asked me on our thirteenth wedding anniversary. We were having dinner at Jake's, one of our favorite restaurants in Del Mar. I'd booked a room at L'Auberge for the weekend, hoping to prove to my wife and myself that thirteen was our lucky number.

"Of course I'm glad," I said. "You're a beautiful and intelligent woman. We have two incredible children. Our life is good."

Dayne nodded slightly and continued eating her salad.

The ocean was calm and the weather was beautiful on that October day, but the weather in Southern California is always beautiful in October. That's why we'd chosen October when we married—it would be beautiful anniversaries for the rest of our lives. Through the large restaurant windows, I watched a family gather the last of their beach items and walk toward their car. The children were young, so there were a variety of sand toys, beach chairs, and paraphernalia. They reminded me of us, and yet they were so different from us. Each family is so much the same and so incredibly different.

"Are you happy you married me?" I asked back after a minute or two.

"Yeah, I guess so," she replied.

I looked directly at her.

"You guess so? Is that what you meant to say?"

"Look, I shouldn't have brought it up," Dayne said in hushed tones. "I don't want to discuss this right now. Can we just eat?"

So that's what we did on our thirteenth anniversary. We paid ninety-eight dollars to eat steak and drink wine in near silence. Of course, we talked about the weather and the height of the waves, because I dredged up some safe topics. We commented about the skill of a surfer and postulated whether Matt or MarLea might surf someday. But the moment a safe topic was exhausted, we returned to our silent and separate worlds.

That night at dinner, my world was filled with simmering frustration that boiled over as soon as we returned to the hotel.

"So you want to tell me what you meant by 'I guess so'?" I demanded, sharpness in my voice.

"Look, Mike, what do you want me to say?" Dayne said sadly. She wasn't mean or harsh or blunt. She was sad.

"I want you to tell me..." I stopped for a few seconds, trying to calm myself. "I want you to tell me what you wouldn't tell me in the restaurant."

"OK then, I will," she said bluntly. "I'm not happy. I thought by now things would be easier...we'd be living in a bigger house, you'd be working fewer hours, we'd travel more. I thought I'd be happier than I am." She paused and took a long breath. "So I guess the answer to your question is I'm not really happy."

"Can I do something to change that?" I asked, trying to sound kind.

"I don't know," she replied, her voice flat and dull. "I'm beginning to think nothing and no one can make me happy."

We sat for a few minutes on the bed, looking out across the pool area. People were in the hot tub. There was celebration and laughter all around, and yet we couldn't manage to capture any for ourselves. I felt like such a failure, looking at my beautiful wife and wishing I could find a way to provide the things that would make her happy.

After a while, I kissed Dayne gently. She didn't push me away. We went for a walk on the beach then came back to our room. I made love to my wife that night, but even I could tell she was just going through the motions.

By physiological standards, our lovemaking was successful. By emotional standards, it fell flat.

Dayne went shopping the next morning. I sat in our room and watched football. She seemed happier when she returned with two sundresses and a pair of shoes. We turned on the radio and drove home, letting someone else provide the lyrics for our anniversary weekend so we didn't have to do it ourselves.

13

IMMEDIATELY FOLLOWING OUR OCTOBER ANNIVERSARY WEEKEND

I'd done a masterful job denying Dayne's growing dissatisfaction for the first thirteen years of our marriage. But now it was out in the open, a daily reminder of my inability to earn her love and my complete incompetence at providing a happy home for my family. For thirteen years I plodded along—fathering, husbanding, working—doing what I'd thought was the right thing. Somehow, fate had determined otherwise. Like an emasculated steer, I'd been blindly walking down a path only to discover it ends in tragedy. I was destined to be hamburger rather than the bull I believed myself to be.

For a while I thought I could reason my way out of the emotion surrounding our anniversary, but whenever I tried to face those particular emotions and deal with them, I discovered only emptiness and a vacuous feeling, as if I'd walked into a deep cave and couldn't escape. Men are supposed to think best in their caves. Usually I do. But it wasn't a cave this time. It was a trap with no escape. I'd put thirteen years into a marriage that was dissatisfying, and I didn't have a clue how to fix the problem. Any clues I'd had were already used up and discarded.

It seemed the best way to cope, at least for the moment, was to stay busy. I avoided conversations with Dayne that included anything bordering on feelings. Frankly, I didn't want to know what she was thinking. It showed on her face most days, and occasionally, it bubbled out of her mouth in the form of vitriolic adjectives. I didn't think of myself as overbearing, ineffective, lazy, selfish, or distant. But apparently Dayne did.

Intelligence should have driven us to counseling. As I describe this now, it's obvious our marriage was in serious trouble. But for some incomprehensible reason, both of us seemed to accept our interactions as a part of life. After all, couples fight, words hurt sometimes, and people disagree. After you'd been married for that long, it was not going to be a bed of roses. It was all part of the cycle of life, wasn't it?

"It's just the normal marital ups and downs," I kept telling myself after each difficult, painful encounter. If I looked to my parents' marriage, it seemed normal. And that was about the only example I could draw on. When the guys got together socially, we talked about business, sports, politics; we didn't talk about the details of marriage. So I had very little idea what went on in other houses, even the homes of my best friends. Even though I seemed to accept this dissatisfied state as normal, somewhere deep inside me, I knew it was unsustainable. The line of gangrene was going to reach a vital organ. Eventually it was going to unalterably damage Dayne or me or our marriage, or all three.

My determination to stay busy worked reasonably well for a while. I focused on work, derived family-based pleasure from interaction with the kids, and found ways to minimize alone time with Dayne. I'd finally learned to read her moods reasonably well. I could tell when she was in a good mood, when she was sexually responsive. And I also became adept at knowing when to come to bed late, when to leave for work early, when to provide space in public. There were times it was just too risky to be in close proximity.

Although it was an effective strategy to minimize conflict, I didn't realize isolation plus hard work would equal trouble. Slowly, feelings I couldn't describe coalesced into a hard ball of irritation and anger. I was tired of reading moods, avoiding conflicts, tiptoeing in my own home. I paid the mortgage. It was my house too.

54

I went for a long drive after work one day through neighborhoods that skirted Pacific Coast Highway. I just didn't want to go home. High on one hill, I sat drumming my fingers on the steering wheel and gritting my teeth as I looked out over the ocean. Sailboats inched along the horizon, following the path of the wind. That's my life, I thought. I'm like a sailboat driven by whatever wind comes by: Dayne's moods, the kids' needs, the latest law passed down by a dysfunctional Congress, the bills that pile onto my desk. The mercurial winds come and demand I follow. My anger grew.

The more I watched those damn sailboats, the more I hated my life. I got out of the car and started walking, just to relieve the mounting rage.

"Screw you," I said into the wind.

It blew back in my face.

"You won't control me," I hissed. "You can't force me."

A small gust picked up a dirty discarded Wendy's bag and hurled it at my leg.

"That all you got?" I threw back as I walked, daring the silence to reveal an answer, not just to my voiced question, but also to the greater questions. I walked for thirty minutes before I realized something. Deep in my heart I knew. No intelligent sailor fights the wind. He will always lose. The wind is stronger than one man, more powerful than an individual. Unless you have additional force to overcome it, you will always go in the direction of the wind.

I got back in my car, feeling like a defeated man. It was impossible to fight these forces without the utter destruction of my family.

"You've got two kids," I told myself silently, the way a responsible parent would have advised me. "It's not about you right now. It's about the kids. Just do the right thing and give these kids a chance for a decent life. When they hit college, you can decide what to do. Just not now."

Somehow those thoughts were comforting. I didn't have to do this forever. Just for now. Just for a few years. I drove home and sat down at the table like a good family man. I smiled and talked to my kids as Dayne served up chicken, rice, salad, and chocolate cupcakes.

14

NOVEMBER, FOURTEENTH YEAR OF OUR MARRIAGE

Rob shocked me one Wednesday morning in November when he walked into my office and told me Leanne had breast cancer.

"I'm going to need a little time off," he said, "while we figure some things out. She may need surgery—chemo for sure."

I got up from behind my desk and grabbed Rob in a strong hug. He and I held each other for a few seconds, and when I moved away from him, he brushed his eyes with the back of his hand.

"I'm here for you, buddy," I said.

"I know."

"Just let me know what I can do."

"Cover for me with a couple of clients. The others can wait, but these two can't."

"Done."

"Thanks."

Rob walked out the door. Mentally, I began calculating. It was only two weeks until Thanksgiving. Typically the holidays weren't our busiest season. Carol had returned, so I knew I could count on her to handle some of the extra workload. I needed to find out about Rob's clients and give Dayne a heads-up.

"Hey, honey," I said as soon as Dayne answered the phone. "I've got some bad news."

"What?"

"Leanne has breast cancer."

"Oh my," Dayne said, genuine concern in her voice. She and Leanne had always gotten along well. "When did they find out?"

"Don't know, but Rob just told me a few minutes ago."

"I'll text her," Dayne said, "and let her know we're praying for her."

Yeah right, I thought. Dayne had a heart for her friends and could show amazing compassion at times, but I'd never heard her pray for anyone. If she actually prayed at all, her prayers were aimed in the direction of an unfamiliar God. If they hit the mark, who knew? Mine were no better.

"I'll be home for dinner tonight, but it may be the last time for a few days," I said. "I'll let you know more when I get home."

Deep in my heart, I knew this was going to be bad. Bad for Leanne, bad for Rob, bad for me, bad for my marriage. I can't tell you why I knew, but I did.

True to form, Dayne was incredibly supportive for the first few days. She talked with Leanne and offered to help with anything. She wrapped me in her arms when I came in late at night exhausted. But Dayne's compassion had a shelf life. It became stale after one week and was discarded within two.

By the time Leanne faced her second round of chemo, Dayne was done with the inconveniences and aiming the full force of her frustration in my direction.

"Damn it, Mike," she yelled one Sunday, "I'm sick of being a single parent."

"What do you want me to do, Dayne?" I shot back. "My partner's not here. He's helping his cancerous wife try to survive. What do you want me to do?" My choice of words appalled me, but I carried my own portfolio of frustration, and it contained some poorly chosen words.

"Have you thought of taking care of your own wife?" she screamed. "Your wife who's exhausted? Why is it you have time to care for Rob's family, Carol's family, everyone's family but ours? You might as well be married to Carol. She sees you more than I do."

I stood silently by our bedroom door for a few seconds then turned and walked downstairs.

"That's just like you, Mike," Dayne said, her voice dripping with disdain. "Walk away. Ignore me. Go back to your precious office. Focus on your business so you never have to come home. It's just like you. Stupid, selfish you."

I walked into my study and sat in silence for a while. There was always just enough truth in Dayne's verbal barbs to make them poison tipped. Poison for the soul. It's impossible to work or think when poison is circulating through your brain, so I sat motionless for some time. Finally, when the sun set and darkness took over the room, MarLea came in. She turned on a light and sat beside me on the couch. Without asking she chose a piano concerto by Felix Mendelssohn, and after we'd listened for a while, lost in our own thoughts, we walked into the kitchen to find food.

15

FOURTEENTH TO SIXTEENTH YEARS OF OUR MARRIAGE

Leanne endured surgeries, chemotherapy, and radiation therapy for nearly two years. Rob came and went—my phantom partner. There today, gone tomorrow, back again. I kept the income steady and watched my home life deteriorate.

It reminded me of the years when our children were babies…constant sleep deprivation, trying to establish routines that felt ineffective as soon as they were implemented. This time everyone involved was exhausted and, above all, deeply concerned that Leanne might not survive. Ultimately, she celebrated the five-year mark cancer-free, but we had no assurances during those long two years, and concern for her survival rode high above all the others.

I had so much on my plate at work that I wasn't around home much. At first Dayne and I fought about it, her accusations growing more pointed with each passing week.

"You're so selfish, Mike. You love sitting at that big impressive desk doing lawyer work while you leave everything else to me."

61

"You think you're high and mighty. You think you're better than me because you have a fancy degree and work in a big office."

"You're the most selfish man I've ever known. You never spend time with your family. You only care about money."

"You think your clients like you, but they don't, Mike. They'd go somewhere else if they knew any other decent lawyers in this town. You're nothing but a paid monkey on the end of their leash. All they do is jerk your chain and you perform. You're pathetic."

I made excuses for these tirades because I knew she was frustrated. I kept telling myself she loved me even as her words cut my ego to shreds. I took it as long as I could, trying to either ignore the pain her words caused or put it away in the vault I had created deep in my soul—a vault to handle the toxic residue of painful accusations. Finally one day I exploded.

"Look, woman," I yelled at her. "Either I keep this freakin' practice going, or we lose it all. The house goes, the cars go, we lose it all. What part of that don't you understand?"

I rarely yelled. In fact, I never yelled. I avoided yelling because I hated being on the receiving end. Dayne was stunned. Her eyes narrowed, and her lips tightened.

"Woman?" she shot back.

"Pick any term you like," I said, my words aimed with precision. "The point remains. I have to work; otherwise everything goes."

"Fine," she said. "Fine." There was a long pause. "I get it." Dayne began to walk away. As she neared the doorway of our bedroom, she looked back at me. It was a look I recognized, but it had a new, harder edge. Her stare was intense, bold, defiant. Her eyes narrowed.

"That's fine, Mike," she said over her shoulder. "You just keep doing what you're doing and see what's left at the end."

"Is that a threat?"

Dayne walked away without answering. As she neared the landing on the stairs, I heard her mumble, "Call it whatever you want."

I kept working, and somehow at the end of those two years, Leanne survived, our practice grew, and I was still married. However, the terms of our marriage had changed. Where I had once had a combative wife and intertwined lives, I now had a distant wife and separate lives. Dayne was fully involved in a life that didn't require my involvement. She had friends at the gym and friends in the kids' carpool. I had work. It was convenient and comfortable, and it looked so blissful when anyone walked by our house. We almost never fought because we were rarely together. If we did fight, Dayne struck with explosive words that tore my self-worth into little shards, so I learned to stay out of her way.

Ours was a marriage concocted by window designers who can position the mannequins precisely. But like mannequins, we had no soul left in our marriage. We moved to a bigger house with an ocean view. We smiled in public and entertained friends with barbecues and dinner parties. We cheered for our children at school events and athletic games. We became window ornaments who got along well because we were facing opposite directions.

It's sad for me to admit this, but these may have been some of our happiest years together.

16

SUMMER, FIFTEENTH YEAR OF OUR MARRIAGE

I hadn't seen Brooke in a very long time. We'd talked on the phone and e-mailed a few times as she completed the business deal, but I hadn't laid eyes on her since the day she touched my arm. Pathetic, isn't it, the realization that I held on to that memory of Brooke's hand on my sleeve? But I did.

And then she arrived in town again, and I offered to pick her up at the airport. It was the perfect opportunity for old friends to catch up over lunch. No harm in that. Dayne would be at her Pilates class, so there was no sense in inviting her to join us. Besides, she hated conversations centered on business.

"It's so great to see you," Brooke said as she slid into the passenger seat of my car.

"You too," I replied. "So how are things in your world?"

"Well…" she said, elongating the word for emphasis. "How much do you want to know?"

I glanced over at her as I changed lanes and headed out of the airport. "Whatever you want to share."

"Mike, I have to be honest. I didn't tell you this on the phone because I was afraid you might bail on lunch. And I wanted to tell you in person."

"OK," I said, my voice filled with curiosity.

"One of the main reasons I'm here is to see Aunt Carol. I need a little advice from her about how to live as a single woman."

"Single?" I asked. Carol had always talked about Brooke and Pete. Pete was her husband. Brooke was married.

"Yeah, single," Brooke said. "Pete decided he didn't want to be married anymore, so he filed for divorce four months ago. I'm just now getting the strength to tell people."

"Why?" I asked impulsively and then immediately reconsidered. "I'm, I'm sorry...it's really none of my business."

"I made it your business when I told you."

"Yeah, I guess you did."

"Well," she said slowly, "I suppose there are many whys in every divorce. Why did we grow apart? Why didn't we do something earlier to save it? Why didn't I see all the signs right in front of my face? Why, why, why..."

"Really, Brooke, you don't have to share anything you don't want to," I said.

"No, I want to talk about this with Aunt Carol, and frankly, I want to talk with you too. Maybe you'll have the male perspective my girlfriends have missed. Maybe you'll find a logical, reasonable way for me to forgive myself and stop looking back."

"Are you blaming yourself?"

"Of course," she said. "The buck stops with Pete and me, and if I blame him then I have to blame myself too."

"Why do you have to blame anyone?" I asked. "Can't it just be a failure without blame?"

"Would any court allow that logic in a disaster?"

"Probably not. But blame is usually assigned to assess financial responsibility."

"Fortunately, we don't have to deal with that," Brooke said. "Pete and I make about the same salary, and we divided the assets down the middle. It wasn't contentious, just painful. Thank goodness no kids were involved. That would have been more complicated."

"So what now?"

"I don't know. I'm not making any changes until there's a compelling reason. I like my job well enough and I found a condo that overlooks a lake and a golf course. It's nice."

"Sounds nice," I said. I waited for a minute to see if she'd say more. She didn't.

We drove and talked about other things until we arrived at my favorite café on Pacific Coast Highway. The hostess led us to a booth. Suddenly I realized how beautiful Brooke was. How the dark walnut of the wooden booth and the green in the upholstery complemented her skin, how attractive she appeared as she laid her jacket beside her and opened the menu. It made me slightly uncomfortable to realize how much I enjoyed looking at her toned arms, her thin fingers, the look of concentration as she studied the menu. I hadn't looked at Dayne like that in years.

The server took our orders, and as soon as he left, Brooke began talking again.

"Mike, if you don't mind sharing..." Brooke hesitated momentarily. "Could you just help me understand why one day Pete was fine being married to me and the next day he wasn't?" She looked down at her fingers, laced together as she brushed one thumb against the other. "I just can't figure out..." She paused—a long, painful pause.

"What?" I asked gently when she couldn't seem to finish the sentence.

"I can't figure out how Pete could make love to me one day and leave me the next." Brooke's tone was soft but somehow strong.

"Maybe he wasn't making love to you," I said as gently as I could. "Maybe he just needed release and you were there."

"If that's true...I could hate him."

"You could."

"Should I?"

"Probably not."

"Why?"

"Because," I said, "hating him won't let you move on with your life. It'll keep you stuck to him."

"Yes," she said. "It would definitely do that." Brooke paused and looked around the room for a moment. "It would also use brain cells I need to use for other things."

I nodded. "Brain cells you definitely need for grocery lists and remembering names at conventions and things like that, which are infinitely more important than Pete."

Brooke smiled. "You're funny, Mike, you know that?"

"I've been told that before."

Brooke reached across the table, squeezed my hand, then let go and returned her hand to her lap. "Thank you for reminding me that hating Pete has no purpose in my life, even if he did hate-worthy things."

"Trust me, Brooke. Nothing good will come out of hating him," I said, my mind focused on the softness of her hand.

"I trust you, Mike. You're right. You're a good man."

We sat for a moment, each with our own thoughts. I don't know what Brooke was thinking, but I was trying to remember the last time Dayne had said I was a good man. I couldn't remember.

As we left the restaurant, I found my hand on the small of Brooke's back, guiding her through an open door. She didn't seem to mind. I opened the car door for her, and she slid into the seat as I stood looking at her legs. Walking around the car, I realized this had just moved from a business lunch to a personal encounter. I didn't open car doors for business associates. I didn't put my hand on the small of an associate's back. Unless I was prepared to have an affair, I had to abort this takeoff.

As we drove toward Carol's house, we talked about politics, law, families. Anything except her marriage or mine. When two people battling bad marriages are in the same space, there's already too much attraction—too much in common. You don't have to increase the chemistry by talking about it.

Carol was still at the office and wouldn't be home for another two hours. I decided to drop Brooke's luggage in the living room and leave quickly. As I set the suitcase down, Brooke walked over and put her hand on my arm.

"Thank you so much, Mike," she said kindly. "I really appreciate your wise words and your kindness. It's a breath of fresh air at a stale time in my life."

"You're welcome," I said as I turned toward the door.

"Would it be out of line if I gave you a hug?" Brooke asked. "You're almost like family to Aunt Carol and to me."

"Of course not," I said, opening my arms to her. The last thing I ever wanted to do was offend Brooke or Carol. Brooke gave me a gentle kiss on the cheek as she hugged me. And then, somehow, I'm not even sure how, the kiss on the cheek became a real kiss. The hug had started completely innocently, a gesture of kindness. The kiss was clearly more. We both stopped suddenly.

"Thanks again for picking me up and for lunch," Brooke said.

"You're welcome," I replied. "Have a great time with Carol."

I started the engine and waved good-bye. The moment I turned the first corner, I realized my thoughts about Brooke were anything but innocent. The next few days were an exercise in self-control.

69

17

BEFORE OUR FIFTEENTH ANNIVERSARY

Carol took two days off while Brooke was in town, so I didn't see either of them except the one time they stopped by the office. Brooke thanked me again for picking her up at the airport. That was it. Then she left.

Summer was filled with work, kids' sports, and the recurring tasks of family life. I still thought about Brooke too much, so as October approached, I decided to make a big deal out of Dayne's and my anniversary, partly because fifteen years is something to celebrate and partly because I felt guilty for kissing Brooke. It shouldn't have happened, and although Dayne didn't know, I still wanted to make it up to her. I booked a trip to Italy. I owed it to my wife. Dayne seemed genuinely excited, and she began reaching out to me in a way I hadn't seen in years. We touched more and began to reconnect the separate lives we'd been leading. It was our summer of love.

As the days turned cooler and the leaves began dropping onto our yard, I found myself working twelve-hour days trying to be sure I didn't leave any cases that would fall heavily on Rob's desk while I was gone. I'd leave the house at six thirty and drive home long after all the rush-hour traffic was securely tucked into garages and parking spaces. I missed dinner every night and usually fell into bed exhausted. I've heard it said that men have only fifty thousand words per day while women use three hundred thousand. By the time I made it home that week, I had no words left. I became a hardworking mute.

Dayne kept things running smoothly at home, so truthfully, I didn't notice how completely detached and silent I'd become until I came home one evening and found Dayne alone and crying. She was sitting in the family room, her feet tucked under her. At first I thought she was looking at something interesting, but as I came closer, I realized she was staring at a wet tissue in her hand. She didn't look up when I reached down to kiss her.

"Is something wrong?" I asked, oblivious.

She didn't answer.

"Dayne, are you all right?"

"No."

"What's wrong?"

The silence filled the room. Then I heard her sniffle.

"Are you crying?"

"Yes."

"Where are the kids?"

"Upstairs."

"Why are you crying?"

Dayne slowly looked up. Her eyes were red, and small smudges of black rested below her eyes. She looked young, and vulnerable, and sad.

"Why are you crying?" I repeated, trying to be gentle through my exhaustion.

Dayne looked at me for another moment without speaking. She hesitated, even after she took a breath and began to speak.

"I'm just...I'm so tired of this."

"Tired of what?"

"Tired of us. Tired of being a married single mother. Tired of never seeing you and then having to act like we're a blissful couple whenever we're in public."

Her words gathered momentum and strength as her voice rose.

"You really think this trip to Italy is going to be wonderful, don't you? You're so stupid. You really think you can ignore me for weeks and years, and then suddenly you'll jet me off to Italy and we'll have this passionate, romantic vacation together." Now her voice discarded the sounds of sorrow and picked up the timbre of accusation.

"You don't want a wife, Mike. You want a blow-up doll. Someone who's there for your pleasure when it's convenient and then stays out of your life the rest of the time. You're too self-absorbed to actually understand a real woman. You just need a toy."

I stood speechless. Her words left me with no capacity to respond. After years of living parallel but separate lives, I thought we could move smoothly from passionate to distant and back again.

"What do you want from me, Dayne?" I finally said. There was more pain in my voice than I expected. "What do you want from me?"

"A marriage," she said flatly.

"I don't know how you define that," I said. "I thought we had one."

"Well, if this is your idea of a marriage, maybe what we need is a divorce," she said.

It was the first time that word had been uttered between us, and it hit the floor with a thud. I'm not naïve enough to believe it hadn't crossed her mind before, or able to deny it hadn't crossed mine, but neither of us had ever given voice to it. Now it was out in the open. What do you do with a live grenade tossed casually into your home? I scrambled through every mental scenario that would diffuse the explosion and decided to throw myself on top of it.

"Oh, baby, I hope you don't mean that," I said sincerely. "Just because I've been an inconsiderate workaholic doesn't mean our marriage is over. You know I love you."

She looked at me, her eyes searching for sincerity. I expected a barrage of accusations, but instead Dayne sat quietly, waiting.

"I promise I'll make it up to you," I continued. "We'll have a great time in Italy. I've planned a few surprises for you—places and experiences you'll love. I know we've been distant for a while, and I don't want that to continue. I truly love you. I want to be a good husband to you. I don't want anything to spoil this trip." I reached for her and she leaned into my arms. "I'll try to be home earlier. Would that help?"

"Yes."

"I'm sorry I've been gone so much. I was just trying to stay ahead of things so they wouldn't follow us to Italy."

I felt her tense and pull away from me slightly. Excuses wouldn't work.

"But I didn't realize how much I was hurting you," I said quickly. Her body relaxed against mine. We sat holding each other for a few minutes until MarLea appeared at the top of the stairs.

"Hey, Dad," she said.

"Hey."

"Do you have time to help me with a math problem?"

"Sure, sis."

Dayne got up and went back into the kitchen. I walked up the stairs to help MarLea. The D-word went back into our closet to hide. I sent Dayne two dozen roses the next day, and they were still beautiful and perky when we left for Rome. They stood tall and proud in their vase on our table, a testament to the strength of a marriage that could survive an errant kiss and a workaholic husband.

18

OCTOBER, OUR FIFTEENTH ANNIVERSARY

Something truly startling occurred to me in Italy. In spite of the magnificent scenery, the luxury hotels, the incredible food—in spite of the perfect setting and the perfect planning—I realized somewhere in the past few years Dayne and I had stopped enjoying each other. We had forgotten how to spend time together, how to enjoy the little personality traits that had once been so attractive. We had lived separate lives for so long that trying to mesh them into a vacation without the padding of another couple or our kids made it feel as though we were playing a high-stakes game of bumper cars. We kept crashing into each other's preferences, habits, and idiosyncrasies. By the end of eight days, we were both irritable and ready to return to our separate lives.

Of course, we didn't say anything to each other. I was determined to make the trip special, and Dayne was determined to create brag-worthy experiences. Her friends would be waiting for the details.

We managed to find a workable method to avoid conflict. Depending on the situation, one or the other of us would give in quickly. Frankly, it was one of the few times I saw my wife willingly sublimate her preferences, but apparently there was a greater goal to achieve. I knew Dayne had talked endlessly with her friends about this trip. She needed the grand finale of a successful and memorable trip. I've often wondered if I was a necessary component of that success or if another girlfriend would have actually been preferable.

From the pictures, you would love our trip: dinners in quaint cafés and family-owned restaurants, tours of magnificent cathedrals and historic cities, vineyards surrounding estates and wineries. But in the quiet of the dining table or the silence of the bed, I came to understand how little Dayne and I had in common. We could talk of the children, my work, our home, but we had nothing else to say. I tried vainly one evening over dinner.

"What did you think of the Coliseum?" I asked after we'd walked the historic section of Rome.

"It was smaller than I expected," Dayne replied. "And in more disrepair."

"Historic sites aren't usually kept up to date," I said, smiling.

"You don't have to be sarcastic," she responded.

"I was just trying to make a joke."

"It wasn't funny."

"OK, then; you decide what we'll talk about."

Dayne paused for a moment. I waited to see what had interested her.

"Do you think we could ask for another pillow at the hotel?" she said.

"Why—do you want two?"

"No, I just want one that's comfortable."

And then I realized we were so completely different. I loved history. Dayne loved comfort. I found her superficiality irritating. She found my humor irritating. We were working our way across Italy rubbing each other the wrong way.

It wouldn't have been so bad, except Brooke kept appearing in my dreams. She would be standing near the Tivoli Fountain or inviting me into a cab outside the hotel. I pushed thoughts of her aside and told myself it was completely inappropriate to be on a trip with my wife and dream about another woman. But truthfully, I knew Italy would be so much more fun with Brooke. She would appreciate my jokes. She would relish the history. She and I wouldn't rub each other the wrong way.

Dayne and I fought the last day we were in Italy. I wanted to make love with the window open, the breeze pouring into our hotel room, the sky looking down on us with its blessing. Dayne was tired and cranky. She missed the kids and her friends.

"Maybe we should just go home," I said in frustration, after trying to entice her into bed. "Maybe we should just get a flight today and end this charade."

"Charade?" Dayne spat in my direction. "Just because you don't always get your way, you're calling our anniversary trip a charade?"

"No," I said, irritated and unwilling to back down. "No, I'm not calling our trip a charade. I'm talking about our marriage."

"You're right," Dayne fired back. "Our marriage is a charade because I'm married to you. You're not a man. You're a hornet and you sting every time you get near me. You're a blind, self-centered jerk who has no idea how much people dislike you. We have no friends because of you!" She paused just long enough to take in a big breath. "If you could just find a way to screw yourself, we'd have the perfect marriage. Leave me alone, I'll do the same to you, and no one will ever know how irritating you are, except maybe a few of my friends, who by the way try to avoid you. Just leave me alone. It'll be better for the kids and it'll save you a fortune in spousal support." She walked abruptly out of the room and didn't return until late that night.

I sat on the balcony of our hotel room until I heard the knob turn. I stared at the city lights. No wonder I dreamed about Brooke. No wonder I worked long hours and avoided coming home. No wonder Dayne and I never talked about anything substantial and made love only once a month—and always in the same position. No wonder.

Dayne and I came home with a camera full of breathtaking photos—after all, we were an attractive couple in a romantic country. Everyone was so happy for us. I would have been, except I was there. I knew the truth. We'd gone to Italy as a couple, and we returned home to our two separate worlds. It was just better that way. It worked for us.

19

NOVEMBER, SIXTEENTH YEAR

The day when you finally admit your marriage is dead is very strange. It doesn't feel good or bad—just dead. I finally stopped denying it two weeks after we returned from Italy. All the signs had been there for months, maybe years. But until that particular Monday, I didn't want to accept them. I wasn't ready. Finally on that Monday, I was. Who can say why one day you won't accept the death of your marriage and the next day you will. Who can say why one day you make love to your wife and the next day you leave her. I have no conclusive answers.

I called Brooke on Wednesday. It probably wasn't my smartest move, but I did it anyway. I felt a little rebellious, being stuck in a dead marriage with no options other than staying or paying spousal support. Rebellion felt good. At least I could do something besides sit there emasculated.

"Hi, Brooke, it's Mike Passick." I wanted to sound like an old friend who just happened to pick up the phone. Brooke was no fool.

"Well, hi there, Mike Passick," she said with a slight playfulness in her voice.

"Do you have a few minutes, or did I catch you at a bad time?"

79

"No." She hesitated and then laughed. "Yes, I have a few minutes. No, you didn't catch me at a bad time."

We both laughed the laugh of the uncertain.

"That's what I get for asking two opposing questions," I said.

"So what's happening in your world?" Brooke jumped in to get the conversation back on track.

"Buried in work, as usual."

"So you just called to chat? Or do you need my expert advice on how to run a legal firm and be wildly successful."

"I can always use that kind of expertise, if you have it," I teased, "but I actually called because I wanted to talk to someone who cared to hear my voice."

"Oh," Brooke said. "That sounds a little sad."

"A little," I said. "But as a man, I'm sworn never to talk about my feelings, so I just wanted to say hi."

"OK," she said. "Hi. Now what do you want to talk about?"

"When are you coming back to Southern California?"

"I've got another meeting in a couple of weeks."

"Would you like to have lunch while you're here?"

"Sure." Brooke's voice had a slight tinge of hesitation.

"Look, no pressure," I assured her. "I just thought it would be nice to see you. Nothing more."

"That would be nice, Mike," she said. "As long as you're comfortable with it, I am."

"Good. Let me know what day works for you and I'll find a nice place for lunch."

We chatted for a few more minutes about work and Carol and life in general. I hung up the phone with a smile on my face. It was true—I just wanted to hear the voice of a woman who wanted to hear mine. It was nothing more than two friends saying hi and planning a nice lunch together. I was pretty sure if I called Dayne and suggested we meet for lunch, she would blow me off. I was tired of that scenario. Time to be around people who enjoyed my company.

Brooke arrived in town two weeks later and we met for lunch in Newport Beach. We ate and talked and flirted a bit, but that was all, so I assured myself it was well within the bounds of my marriage vows. Really no different from a business lunch, except for the fact there was so much chemistry in the air, it seasoned the food and made every bite melt in my mouth. I gave Brooke a perfectly appropriate hug and opened her car door as she left for her meeting.

Then I called her the next morning just to chat.

I wasn't entirely certain why I wanted to talk to Brooke every day when I had no desire at all to talk with Dayne. Probably because Dayne had no interest in my business, my life, or my interests. Whenever I shared any of those, she responded with a litany of her own problems and how I was no support at all. Talking with Brooke was like drinking fresh water from a spring after living on stale water for years. It was life giving, energizing. It gave me a reason to get up in the morning.

So Brooke and I found ourselves talking on the phone many mornings. Talking about art or movies or work or anything. Just talking in order to gather strength to face the reality of our lives: one of us a fresh divorcée and the other stuck in a dying marriage. Two survivors clinging to hope in the form of conversation.

20

DECEMBER, SIXTEENTH YEAR

Two weeks before Christmas, I got caught in a massive traffic jam and arrived at work just after ten. I was usually at my desk much earlier, and as I walked through the door, I expected to see the signs of a busy office. Instead I was greeted by an empty front desk and silence. Rob's door was shut, so I went to my office and launched into the day's paperwork. A few minutes later, Rob appeared at my office door looking very serious.

"Mike, do you have a few minutes?"

"Sure."

"I need you to come into my office and speak with Carol and me."

"OK."

I pushed my chair back and followed Rob into his office. Carol was sitting in a chair looking out the window. Her eyes were red and puffy. It was clear she'd been crying. I looked at Rob questioningly, and he motioned for me to take a seat.

"Mike," Rob said slowly, "there's no easy way to say this, so I'll just say it. Carol has been embezzling from us."

I could feel my heart speed up and hear a slight buzzing in my ears. I looked at Rob then at Carol. Rob turned to face me directly. Carol kept

83

looking out the window. I was aware of the need to swallow, and I felt my hands clench and unclench.

"I know this is a shock," Rob continued, "so I'll just tell you what I know and then let Carol talk with both of us before we determine how to handle this.

"As you and I agreed, I scheduled an independent audit of our records. Our accountant has always received all the information through Carol, so I had no reason to suspect there would be any issues with financial records. We've never had any reason to doubt Carol's honesty or loyalty to our firm.

"This morning I arrived at the office a little earlier than usual and had a voice mail from the auditor asking me to call his cell phone right away. He had questions about cash payments I couldn't answer, so I looked through a couple of Carol's files and opened some computer records. It took a bit of looking, but I found that over the course of the last few years, Carol has taken what she terms 'short-term loans' totaling more than forty thousand dollars. Some have been paid back. Many have not."

I sat perfectly still, except for the rise and fall of my chest and the slight jerking motions of my left foot I couldn't seem to stop. I glanced over at Carol, who was now crying silently with her eyes on the floor.

"Frankly, Mike, I'm at a loss for words. Carol has admitted to taking the money, but said she has always intended to pay it back."

"I did," Carol said suddenly, looking at me with pleading eyes. "I really did, Mike. You have to believe I never intended...I would never...steal from you and Rob."

"I know," I thought, without realizing the words would actually come out of my mouth.

"Before we say anything else," Rob interjected, "we need to talk—you and me."

"Yes," I agreed. "We need to talk."

"Carol," Rob said, "I want to give you a chance to talk with both of us and help us understand what happened here. Then I'm going to ask you to leave while we discuss the next step."

Carol nodded. I sat quietly. I was beginning to get my bearings, beginning to see the reality of the situation. Our loyal employee had been dishonest. Brooke's aunt was a thief. Another woman in my world had shown her true colors. The anger began to rise. Rob saw my body language change and leaned toward me.

"Mike, I know this is a lot to process at once, but let's let Carol talk for a few minutes, and then we'll talk, OK?"

"Sure," I said. "That's a good plan."

Carol cleared her throat, dabbed her eyes with a tissue, and looked out the window again for a few seconds.

"I don't know what to say," she began. "You guys have been nothing but kind to me. You've always treated me like family, especially since J. C. died. I would never knowingly hurt you, but I..."

Her voice broke and she stopped talking for a bit.

"I didn't know what to do. After J. C. died, I had to wait for his life insurance money, so I just borrowed a little one month for my mortgage payment and I paid it back within a week. Then quite a few months later, you remember..." She looked up to see if there was any sign of sympathy in our eyes. She might have seen some, but then she looked away again. "You remember when my transmission had to be replaced in the same month as the trip to help my sister. I just didn't have the money to pay for both of them. I had to have my car, and I had to help my sister after her surgery."

Carol's voice was pleading, and it hurt me to hear her begging us for mercy, as if she were on trial, about to face execution at the hands of a judge. Then it hit me. We were talking felony here. She was pleading for her freedom.

"I paid that back too, but it took longer, and then J. C.'s medical bills came and one of my kids lost his job for six months and needed money and my house had a slab leak, and all of a sudden I couldn't keep up with paying it back. That's when I realized I was in trouble.

"I thought about talking to you, but I realized you didn't know and I thought I could get it all paid back before you did." Carol's voice broke again and tears ran down her cheeks. "I'm sure you think I'm crying because I got caught, but the truth is I'm crying because I really care about you both and I feel so bad about this whole thing."

There was silence in the room. Rob and I had been attorneys too long to take words at face value. Words could be used to manipulate, to plead for sympathy, to distract. Words could be the greatest weapon of all when used by a skilled combatant. The question was, were we in a fight, or were we on the same side? I wasn't sure.

"Would you like to say anything more, Carol?" Rob asked.

"Is there anything else we should know?" I leaned toward her ever so slightly. *Please,* I was thinking, *please tell us something that makes this palatable. I don't want to lose you. You're the only receptionist and office manager we've ever had. You're the only woman I've ever really trusted.*

"No," Carol said quietly. "That's all I can say. It's the truth. I never intended to take your money or to hurt you."

Suddenly, I felt the need to step up and be part of the leadership in the room. Suddenly, I didn't want to be viewed as the weaker partner, the shell-shocked one. I wanted to be strong.

"Carol," I said, "why don't you go home and wait for our call. You may take any personal items you need from your desk, but you are not to touch your computer or any records. We'll call you in a few hours."

"OK," Carol said. She picked up the notepad she'd brought into Rob's office and walked out of the room the same way she always did after any other meeting. It was familiar and sad. I realized there's no way to maintain dignity when you've broken trust, when your life has changed forever and you have to walk out. You can only hope your retreating view shows strength because it will not have dignity.

I walked with Carol to her desk, where she picked up her purse, her coat, and a tube of hand cream from the top drawer.

"We will call you in a few hours," I said as I closed the front door behind her.

I walked back into Rob's office and sat down hard in the chair. Rob had his head in his hands and his elbows resting on his desk. He didn't look up right away, so I sat looking out the window silently.

"Didn't expect that," I said after a few minutes of silence. Rob lifted his head and nodded. "What do you think we should do?"

"Not a clue," Rob replied.

"We have options," I said.

"Sure we do," Rob shot back, "but I don't like any of them. We can turn her in and she'll become a felon. Or we can bring her back and forever wonder if she's being honest with us. We can hire someone else and wonder if they'll do the same thing or something worse." Rob slammed his hand down on his desk with such anger the windows rattled. "I don't want to hire someone else, Mike. I like Carol."

"Yeah, I get that. Me too."

We sat there another minute in silence. Then Rob spoke.

"I can't think right now. I'm going to go to the gym and blow off some steam. How about if we meet in a couple of hours and try to figure this out."

"Works for me," I said.

Rob gathered his things and left quickly. I knew an hour or two in the gym would help him, and I was grateful for the chance to be alone in the office. I picked up the phone and realized suddenly there was no one to call. Talking with Dayne would just make things worse. Talking with Brooke would add another layer of complication.

I can truly say I never felt more alone in this world than at that moment. Isn't this what companionship and marriage and friendship and caring are supposed to be for? When you're drowning and you need someone on shore with a lifeline. I didn't have a lifeline. I had a dead marriage and a hidden friendship. Neither was comforting in this situation. I was alone.

21

DECEMBER, SIXTEENTH YEAR

I walked around the office for a few minutes, trying to decide whether to stay or leave. The phone rang a few times and I let it go to voice mail. The office was closed. We were out. Don't call.

I tried to focus on paperwork, but I kept picturing Carol's face looking out the window. Was she sad, caught, worried, grief stricken? What exactly was I seeing on her face? After thinking about that for a few minutes, I realized it didn't matter. No matter what emotion she was feeling, I couldn't consider that right now. She'd been caught embezzling from us. She had betrayed our trust. She was stealing from us. All the contrition in the world didn't change that fact.

Boy, I can sure pick 'em, I thought to myself. Three women have dominated my life: my mother, spineless and fragile; my wife, distant and self-absorbed; and my office manager, dishonest and untrustworthy. I felt another surge of anger, followed closely by a deep desire to escape. Who would miss me if I packed up everything and moved? Rob would get another partner, and Dayne would be dating within days. Maybe my kids would miss me. Maybe. Before I could play with that idea any longer, my cell phone rang.

"Mike." It was Brooke. "Will you talk to me?"

"Why wouldn't I?"

"My aunt just called me. I know what happened."

"Why did she call you?"

"She knows you and I talk from time to time. She knows we're friends."

"Oh."

"Will you talk to me?"

"Look, Brooke, I need to talk with my partner first. It's really an internal matter. Although I understand your concern, I have to talk with Rob first."

"I understand," Brooke said softly. "I was just hoping you weren't going to call the police. My aunt is distraught. She is so afraid."

"She has reason to be, Brooke," I said, a little stronger than I intended. "She's stolen a lot of money."

I expected Brooke to fire back, the way I knew Dayne would have in the same situation. I braced for a barrage of words. They didn't come. There was only silence for a few seconds.

"Yes, Mike," Brooke said. "You're right. She has stolen a lot of money. But I'm just asking for one small favor. Would you please allow me to talk with you and Rob before you make any final decisions? Would you just allow me that?"

I hesitated for just a moment, not knowing exactly how to respond.

"Mike?" Her voice was soft, pleading.

"Yes."

"Please let me talk to you and Rob sometime today. Don't call any authorities until we talk, OK?"

"OK."

"Thank you, Mike."

"Sure." I waited a few seconds to see if she would hang up first. She didn't. I sat in silence, listening to the hum of electronics all around me. Brooke still did not hang up. She waited silently.

"Listen, Brooke..." The sigh that came out after those words surprised me. It was a heavy sigh from deep within me. "Rob has gone out for an hour or two. We're both really shaken by this, and we're just trying to pull ourselves together before we make any decisions. When he gets back, I'll see if he's willing to talk with you. No promises, but I'll see. OK?"

"Of course. I'll wait to hear from you," Brooke said.

"I'd much rather talk with you about the new exhibition at the Getty," I said, trying to lighten the mood.

"Yeah, me too," Brooke said sadly. "Remember, Mike, I'm shaken too. This is my favorite aunt we're talking about."

"I get that. She's my favorite office manager. She's the nicest dishonest person I know."

"I don't think she meant to steal anything from you."

"Does that matter?" My voice was tense, sharp.

"No," Brooke said softly. "Not really, unless you consider motive to be part of her defense."

"The jury's out on that one," I said.

"OK…well…please call me when you and Rob can talk. I have to be honest, Mike, I want to keep my aunt out of jail."

"I'll call you and we'll see what we can do."

I hung up the phone slowly. It was marginally comforting to hear Brooke's voice, but not as comforting as I wanted it to be. I thought she might push, insist, pressure me. She hadn't. I wasn't used to that approach, and it made me slightly uncomfortable.

Rob walked through the door an hour or so later. His hair was wet and his face was ruddy. He'd pushed his body hard in an effort to gain clarity. I'd done nothing in an effort to gain time. I didn't want to face this discussion, but it couldn't be avoided.

"So what do you think we should do?" Rob began, wiping a trickle of sweat from the side of his neck.

"Hire a good attorney?" I said, trying to be funny.

Rob smiled halfheartedly.

"I don't know, Rob," I said. "I'm certainly not ready to take legal action against her, nor am I ready to welcome her back with open arms as if nothing happened."

"I agree with both those statements," Rob said. "So if those are off the table, then what are other options?"

"Rehab?"

"Great idea. I wonder if the Betty Ford Center has a six-week program for embezzlers." Rob shook his head and gave me a weak smile.

"Seriously, Rob," I said, "is she rehabable? Was this a problem that, once discovered, can be managed well enough to keep her as our office

91

manager? Even though I'm shocked and hurt and frustrated, I don't really want to lose her."

"It's bizarre, Mike," Rob replied. "I don't want to lose her either. I'm just not sure how to handle something this serious without firing her. That's what I'd do for anyone else who stole from us. If I caught someone stealing a box of paper, or a computer, or anything, I'd fire them. She stole a lot more than that."

"Yeah, she did. There's no denying the facts. The question for me remains is Carol a good person who made a very bad mistake, or is she a bad person who finally got caught?"

"Motive?"

"Yeah, we have to consider motive, or we can't possibly determine our own course of action."

Rob and I sat thinking for a bit, and then I spoke.

"I got a call from Carol's niece while you were at the gym."

Rob looked at me questioningly. "And…"

"She wants us to call her before we make any final decision."

"Call her?"

"Yes. Carol must have called her right after she left the office, and Brooke would like us to call her before we decide on any action. She clearly wants to avoid any criminal charges against her aunt, so she'd like us to call her."

"Should we?"

"I can't see why not," I said. "All we have to do is listen. She has no vote in the outcome, but she may be able to give us additional information that will make our decision clearer."

"All right," Rob said. "We could use additional information. I feel no certainty in any outcome right now."

I picked up the office phone, punched the speaker button, and dialed Brooke's number. She answered on the third ring.

"This is Brooke Westin."

"Hi, Brooke, this is Mike. Rob and I are calling as you requested."

"Thank you," Brooke said, relief and strength in her voice. "I really appreciate your willingness to talk with me. Thank you so much. Let me just shut my office door." Rob and I sat in silence while Brooke rustled in the background.

"Thanks," she said. "Thank you for waiting."

"So, Brooke," Rob began, "I assume you know the situation."

"I know the basics. My aunt has been borrowing without authorization from your cash payments and reserves, and over the course of the last three years, she's misdirected about forty thousand dollars. Is that right?"

"That's what we discovered," I said.

"So my basic facts are correct?"

"Yes," Rob answered. "Those are the basics."

"First," Brooke said, "may I ask if you are willing to work this out without criminal charges being filed?"

"If that's a feasible option, I think we'd be willing to consider it," I said, turning to see if Rob agreed. He was nodding. "Carol has done many things right as our office manager. We're stunned by this betrayal, but we don't have an overwhelming desire to punish her through the judicial system."

"I'm relieved to hear that," Brooke said. "I honestly believe my aunt made a mistake. A regrettable, distasteful, and dishonest mistake, but one born of no ill motives toward either of you."

"We don't doubt that, Brooke," Rob said. "But we still have to deal with the breach of trust."

"I completely understand," Brooke replied. I found myself marveling at her strength, her willingness to risk our anger, her lack of defensiveness. I had not seen Brooke in a negotiation before, and I suddenly realized she was quite good at it. "There are two very distinct issues here. One involves monetary loss and the other involves loss of trust. May I speak to why these are connected?"

"Of course," Rob said quickly.

"Please understand I am not making any excuses or suggesting this should be swept under the rug. I am only trying to provide context for my aunt's actions so that you can arrive at the best decision." Brooke paused for moment. "My uncle and aunt had a very traditional marriage for their generation. J. C. took care of all the finances while he was alive, so when he died so suddenly, my aunt Carol was left to decipher budgets and financial matters alone. Her children are loving and caring, but they are not trained in finance, so their advice to her was minimal and often ineffective for her situation. One of the reasons I have come to California these last three years was to help her with particularly large financial decisions, but I had no idea she was unfamiliar with the basics of budgeting. I honestly thought her

93

kids or some of her friends were all the resources she needed for financial decisions. Obviously, I realize now, that was a serious mistake on my part. You see, my aunt is a proud woman who was unwilling to admit to anyone, including her children and me, that she needed help."

Brooke paused again. I couldn't tell if she was trying to control her emotions or if she was giving the words time to sink in. Either way, I was listening.

"Her pride put her in this untenable situation, and instead of asking for help, which frankly, any of us would have gladly given her, she simply handled it the only way she could think of. She took, to use her words, 'short-term loans,' and because her budgeting skills were weak to begin with, she got in very deep very quickly.

"So," Brooke continued, "that leaves us with this nasty situation."

Rob and I looked at each other silently. I nodded.

"If you would allow me to suggest a solution, I believe I have one that might solve many problems and allow my aunt to continue working, which she so enjoys, either at your office or at another. Your choice."

"If you have that solution, Brooke," I said, almost too quickly, "you will be the miracle worker we've been looking for."

"Here's what I propose," she said. "My aunt still owes you…about how much?"

"About twenty-three thousand dollars," Rob answered.

"OK, twenty-three thousand. Would you be willing to consider that an eighteen-month loan to me and allow me to pay it back on her behalf?"

"To you?" I was shocked. Rob looked confused.

"Yes, to me."

"Why?"

"Because I have the resources to pay it and I think her kids will pitch in too. I believe it is a small price to pay for my aunt's education regarding money. Call it her tuition in the school of hard knocks."

I smiled. Brooke was a skilled communicator. She hadn't lost us yet.

"That would take care of your monetary loss," she continued, "but we still have to address the loss of trust."

"Yes," I said. "That's also a deep concern."

"I understand. I'm sure I would feel the same if I were in your shoes," Brooke said without hesitation. "So let me propose this. My aunt has done

94

good work for you and has been an asset to your practice for many years. Aside from this lapse in judgment, she has been a good employee, correct?"

"We're listening," Rob said.

"I believe this entire mess occurred because my aunt has not been given the tools to manage her money well. In the last hour, I've found a seminar near her home that provides a basic education in personal money management. It covers things like cash flow, retirement planning, proper use of credit cards, and budgeting for large expenses such as replacing cars and appliances. I believe whether or not Aunt Carol continues to work for you, she needs to take this class. No one has taught her how to budget. She needs to learn.

"I'm also willing to help her find a counselor. She needs to see someone regularly for a while to be certain she deals with the guilt and shame, and to provide clear direction as to how she can regain trust in the workplace, whether that's at your office or at another job."

Rob and I sat quietly listening as Brooke spoke. It was clear she'd thought this out carefully and had hopes we would not reject her ideas without consideration. My first reaction was agitation. Now I had another woman's feelings to consider if we fired Carol. I was a little irritated at myself for allowing Brooke to become part of this. I should have just let her be Carol's support when we fired her and she was out looking for work again. She needed to be fired. You couldn't just steal from a business and go right back to work the next day. It was not right.

Rob looked at me when it was obvious Brooke had finished her pitch. I looked back at Rob and gave him the "I don't know what to say" look. Rob gave me the same look back.

"I know you need to talk and make a decision," Brooke said after the pause. "I just wanted to share this information with you. I ask you to consider whether it's in the best interest of my aunt, whom we all care for, and the best interest of your firm, which we all care for, to fire her and start with someone unknown. There is no guarantee with a new employee."

She paused for a moment to let that realization sink in. She was right. Rob and I had picked Carol, and she embezzled from us. Who was to say we wouldn't pick another dishonest employee?

"I truly believe this was a mistake," Brooke continued, "not a malicious act, and I am willing to make full restitution. I also believe she can continue to be an outstanding employee for you if you will give her a second chance."

"Thank you, Brooke," I said in the most professional voice I could muster. I didn't want to be a friend right now. I wanted to feel some distance and safety. "Rob and I will talk it over. Thank you again for sharing your perspective."

"Thank you for listening," Brooke said.

Rob and I sat in our own thoughts for a few minutes after we hung up. Neither of us spoke, because frankly, there wasn't anything worth saying. It didn't feel right to make Brooke pay for Carol's actions. It didn't feel right to be discussing how to fire Carol. Nothing felt right. Most of all, going home did not feel right.

"I can't think right now," Rob said finally. "I need to sleep on it and go work out some more. I need perspective and I don't have any right now."

"Me either," I agreed.

"Look, if you don't have anything pressing, let's take the rest of the day to regroup. I'll be back tomorrow morning. We can figure it out then."

"Works for me," I said. "Nothing on my desk will explode before tomorrow."

Rob started to walk out of my office.

"Hey, Rob."

"Yeah?"

"Are you going to talk with Leanne about this?"

"Probably. Why?"

I paused. I'd managed to keep my marital problems out of the office, and now didn't seem like the best time to insert them. Rob kept looking at me.

"I don't know if I'll share this with Dayne," I said. "She has a lot on her plate with the kids, and I don't want to add to her stress." Rob nodded. I looked down. It was a bald-faced lie. I didn't want to share anything with Dayne, not because of her stress level, but because I was sure any communication on my part would be greeted with accusation and derision. We'd just end up in a fight. I didn't want any more fights or blame or communication. I just wanted Dayne to leave me alone.

Rob turned toward the front door. "I'll ask Leanne to keep it completely confidential," he said as he walked out. "Don't worry. She will."

"Thanks," I said. "I'll see you tomorrow around eight."

Rob left quickly. For the first time I could remember, he didn't take his Tumi bag or his laptop or anything from his desk. He just left.

I sat in my office for a few minutes before I realized I had nowhere to go. No one to call, nowhere to go. All I knew was I had to leave the office. It was only noon, and I had to get out. I just wasn't sure where I would go.

22

DECEMBER, SIXTEENTH YEAR

I got in my car and simply started driving. North on the 405. I didn't know where I was going, but I knew I was getting the hell out of Dodge. It felt as if bullets were flying in our office—somebody was going to get hurt—and I had every reason to believe bullets would fly at home too. Dayne wasn't stupid. She'd figure out something was wrong; she'd push me to tell her, and then the blame and arguing would begin. Better to avoid that gunfight.

I drove through Los Angeles, past the Getty, through the valley. I stopped in Camarillo at the outlet malls and bought myself a golf shirt, socks, and a pack of men's briefs. A pharmacy nearby had an entire section of "I forgot it at home" supplies in small containers. I bought fifteen dollars' worth and then kept on driving. Past Santa Barbara through Pismo Beach all the way to San Luis Obispo. I was low on gas, so I drove into town, filled up, and found a parking space on Higuera Street. Trees and stores lined both sides, quaint stores with unique window displays and racks of clothes outside. Completely different from the retail centers near my office. This town was like an oasis. Cool, unrushed, filled with college students drinking coffee at sidewalk tables and professorial types walking briskly. Ah yes, now I remembered. SLO was a college town. That was why.

I sat in the car for a while, waiting for some kind of inspiration to get out or to drive. Nothing hit me except jumbled thoughts. During the drive, I hadn't allowed myself to think. I'd been blasting AM talk radio, listening to the problems of politicians and sports figures to keep my mind off my problems. Now the noise was off and thoughts bounced off the surface of my brain like hail. The sun had already dipped behind the hills. It was nearly five o'clock. I realized I needed to call home eventually. I sat for another few minutes then picked up my phone. MarLea answered on the third ring.

"Hi, kid."

"Hi, Dad."

"Your mom there?"

"Yeah, just a second."

MarLea began calling for Dayne. In a few seconds I heard Dayne's voice. "What's up?"

"Hey, I just wanted to let you know I got called out of town on business. I won't be home tonight."

"Really? Tonight?" Dayne sounded pissed.

"There a problem?" I asked.

"Mike, you could have let me know," Dayne began. "You never mentioned you were going out of town, so I made plans for tonight, thinking you could drive MarLea to her game at seven. You're really not coming home at all? And you didn't bother to let me know before now?"

"I'm sorry, Dayne..." I began, but she cut me off.

"How the hell do you expect me to run this house if you don't ever communicate with me?" Her voice was getting louder. I stayed quiet. "How do you think I feel when you do whatever you want and leave me to pick up the pieces?"

I stayed silent.

"Answer me, Mike," Dayne yelled into the phone. "What am I supposed to do about tonight since you're off on some lousy trip? Why don't you just explain to MarLea why you can't be here for her and she'll have to hitch a ride like some orphan while her dad abandons her?"

"Look, Dayne, I'm sorry. It couldn't be helped."

"Sure," she said flatly.

"Can you manage to get MarLea to her game?"

100

"Of course," she said, her voice dripping with sarcasm. "I'll just let my friends know they can go to the theater without me again. It's not the first time your selfishness created problems for me."

I stayed silent. There was nothing to say. I was already emotionally drained, and to hear Dayne berate me because she was going to miss time with her friends was almost too much to believe. I wanted to tell her "You have no idea what I've been through." I wanted to give her an earful of what my day had been like. I wanted her to understand missing the theater would be a walk in the park compared with the decisions I faced about Carol. In years past, I might have tried, I might have really wanted to talk about it, but now I just stayed silent.

"You are so stinkin' selfish, Mike," Dayne spat into the phone. "You never think of anyone but yourself."

"Yep...that's me," I said suddenly. And I hung up. I'd never hung up on my wife before. It was something I abhorred—hanging up on people. I had vowed many years ago I'd never do it to anyone I loved. And yet I'd just hung up on Dayne, and I felt no remorse. I was driving north, lying to my wife about some made-up business trip, and I'd just hung up on her. I felt nothing but relief.

The phone rang. I ignored it till it went to voice mail. It rang again and again. Voice mail. Finally it stopped ringing.

I got out of the car and started walking. A nice-looking woman smiled at me as I walked by. Screw her. I wanted nothing to do with women right now. They were nothing but trouble. *Just leave me alone. I don't want your attention. I don't want to communicate with you. I don't want to do anything but escape from you.*

My phone rang again. This time I looked at the number. It was Brooke. I let her call go to voice mail too. I had nothing to say to any of the women in my world. They were all just trouble, filling my life with frustration. I couldn't trust any of them.

The chilly air drove me into a nearby door. My eyes landed on a long wooden bar displaying bottles and glasses. Voices and bodies, sounds and smells surrounded me. Long brightly colored cylinders of varying sizes hung on the wall, probably a local artist's work. They looked to me like oversize wind chimes covered with fluorescent graffiti. People were everywhere—sitting at small tables, talking at the bar, standing in small groups.

A few turned to look, but I wasn't ready to make eye contact. I just stood with my back to the brick wall, lost in my own thoughts about escape. If I had to escape, I'd definitely picked the right town. My senses were wide awake.

"How many in your party?"

I looked around at the young woman in black with a string of holiday ornaments around her neck. She was clearly waiting for an answer.

"Would you like to be seated for dinner?" she asked.

Only then did I realize I was in front of the hostess and I was hungry.

"One," I said.

"I can seat you now."

I followed her past the bar, along a narrow hall that paralleled the kitchen, toward the back of the restaurant. Rich smells curled around me in the hallway—smells of potatoes, bread, steak, and caramelizing sugar. I kept my eyes on the hostess and her swaying black skirt as we snaked past the noisy kitchen to a patio out back. Trees branches decorated in white lights bowed deeply over the tables. Candles flickered, completing for attention with the last bit of the sunlight. The hostess directed me to a corner table facing the other diners and the trees along the stream. I couldn't hear any water, but somehow I could feel the calm of its presence. I felt as if I'd climbed into my own private tree house, complete with a chef and wait staff. If I ever needed a tree house, it was now.

A redhead named Ashley took my drink order. Her arms were strong and defined. It made me wonder what sport she played, but I was too disengaged and exhausted to ask. I ordered a glass of a San Genovese blend and sat looking at the luxuriant foliage as I relished the wine from the first sip to the last. It went perfectly with the empanada appetizer I savored slowly and the fillet I could almost cut with my fork. By the time I'd taken the last bite, my stomach was content and my mind was beginning to relax.

"Can I interest you in dessert tonight?" Ashley asked when she noticed my plate was empty.

"I don't think so. Thank you." I smiled at her and realized MarLea would be her age in just a few years. I wasn't the age of wait staff anymore. I was the age of managers, professors, fathers.

"I'll be right back with your check," Ashley said.

I watched her walk away. Maybe that's what I needed. Someone young. Someone energetic. Someone to take my mind off my troubles. It was a fleeting thought. I'd lived long enough to know you couldn't run from or screw your way out of trouble. You might temporarily distance yourself with a new car or a toned body next to you in bed. But trouble had an amazing way of stalking and overtaking everyone on that path, leaving only gutted carcasses behind.

I paid the bill when Ashley returned and slowly made my way back toward the front of the restaurant. The bar area was even more crowded now. There seemed to be many more people my age. I stopped for a moment and leaned against the wall, surveying the room. With very little effort, I realized, I could probably enjoy a terrific night with a nice-looking woman. This town seemed to have more than its fair share of attractive women. I wasn't a man who had to have a co-ed. I could well enjoy the company of a woman closer to my age. After all, I'd enjoyed Brooke's company. Why not an educated, interesting, fascinating woman of the Central Coast? Within seconds of that thought, I noticed a dark-haired, professionally dressed woman looking in my direction. Our eyes met. She smiled then looked away. All I needed to do was walk over and start a conversation. It would be so easy. It would feel so good to be with someone who desired me. I could probably get laid right here in this quaint little town without much effort.

My mind juggled thoughts like a circus performer. *You're a married man who's dealing with serious stress...why not relax and take a little risk...no, don't add to your problems...come on, enjoy yourself before you have to go back...no, walk away...walk away, Mike, walk away.*

The cool outside air wrapped around my face and slithered under my jacket. I pushed my hands deeply into my pockets and started walking. It felt rote, rhythmic, automated. There was no bounce in my step, but the concrete that had glued me to the floor of my office earlier had begun to break away. I walked for about an hour—up one side of Higuera Street, past an African-themed art gallery and the open doors of conversation-filled restaurants, across Santa Rosa Street with smells of barbecue and beer, over to Broad, and then back along Higuera toward the Mission. I sat down on a rock wall near the upper level of the Mission and looked over the greenery and holiday decorations below.

"What are you doing, Mike?" I asked myself. "Who are you and what are you doing?"

That was a good question.

Through the fog of the stress, the thoughts about sex, and the unresolved issues surrounding the women in my life, I started to think about that one question. Who am I?

All I'd ever been was the good guy. My brother bailed out of the family as soon as he could, but I stayed because I always felt compelled to do the right thing. I dealt with my father's funeral, I stayed in a difficult marriage, I worked to support my wife and kids, I stepped back from a kiss with Brooke. And what did it get me? A woman at home who hated me. An employee who stole from me. A world that had me at a table eating by myself. Yeah, that was some payoff for a good life—a great reward for being a good guy.

The cool damp rock wall was beginning to seep through my pant legs, so I started walking again.

Maybe this good living was just a big cosmic joke. Maybe I should walk back into that bar and find someone enjoyable to remind me there could still be excitement in life. Maybe I should just keep driving and leave it to Rob to figure out a solution at work. Maybe I should serve Dayne with divorce papers and let her figure out how to survive without the energy of her constant anger toward me. Maybe it was finally time to quit being the good guy and let someone else take over as Captain America.

Somehow I'd managed to walk full circle. I was standing in front of the bar again. The same attractive brunette was now sitting at a table near the front window, talking with another woman. She looked up just as I saw her and smiled my direction. It wasn't a bold smile. It didn't beg or seduce. It simply called to me with the word *hi*. I felt compelled to answer.

I walked toward her table, and she greeted me with a smile. "Would you like to join us? There's an extra seat at our table."

"Sure," I replied.

"I'm Olivia. This is Megan. We work at the university."

"Hi, I'm Mike. I'm an attorney from down south."

"How far south?" Megan asked in a playful tone. "You're not representing drug cartels in Mexico, are you?"

"Ah…no." I smiled back. "Just business clients in SoCal. Nothing too exciting, unless you count embezzling."

"Embezzling?" Olivia shot back.

"Yeah."

"An employee or a client?"

"An employee," I said flatly. "But hey, let's talk about something more interesting than my life. Maybe something like politics or religion to really get the party started."

The women laughed. I hadn't lost it yet. I looked down at my wedding ring. Then I noticed Olivia had one too.

"So Megan and I were just discussing the pros and cons of small-town life," she said, clearly aware I had noticed her marital status. "Do you like the big city, or do you think a town like SLO has something special to offer?"

I looked directly into her eyes. Brown, with spots of green and gray. Pretty.

"Depends what you're looking for," I responded. "Tonight I was looking for a warm place with interesting people. I think I found it."

"I think you did," Olivia responded quickly. I thought I saw her wink.

The three of us chatted for another twenty minutes, and then Megan offered a convenient excuse to leave and suddenly Olivia and I were sitting at the table alone.

"So, Mike," she said, cradling her drink between her thumb and fingers, gently rubbing the side of the glass. "What are you really looking for in SLO tonight?" She let her voice trail off seductively. I looked at her. She was a pretty woman, intelligent, fun, sultry. Her clothes fit nicely around her curves. Her smells were inviting. She could be a wonderful distraction.

"I don't know."

"Maybe someone to take your mind off all the things that are troubling you?"

"Maybe," I said.

"So what do you propose?"

I thought for a few moments. The offer was so tempting. No one would ever know. No one but me. I would know. I would become one of those men who lied to his wife and betrayed his children, who lived as two people and stared at a divided face in the mirror every morning.

105

"I should go, Olivia. You're a very interesting and beautiful woman. But I'm not ready to introduce more complications into my life." The good guy surfaced again. No matter how many times I tried to let my defiant side come up, he was always pushed under by the good guy. Was it in my genes, my training, my beliefs? A piece of me was angry, but a larger part of me was relieved.

"I need to say good night," I continued. "Thanks for an enjoyable conversation."

Her face fell, but she maintained an air of professional composure.

"You must have a lot on your mind," she said softly.

"I do."

"I hope it works out for you."

"Believe me, a lot of things need to work out."

"Drive safely, Mike."

"Thanks," I said as I stood up. There was nothing left to say, so I walked out the door and down the street. My car had a layer of moisture on the windshield. Time to get in, warm it up, and drive. I found a hotel two exits away and carried my outlet bags into the lobby. A room on the third floor would be great. By the time I crawled into bed, I was too tired to set an alarm. I don't remember falling asleep that night. I just remember I did. A deep sleep punctuated by dreams of drowning and sex.

106

23

DECEMBER, SIXTEENTH YEAR

The hardest part of running away is determining your destination. If you don't have something to run to, you might as well just go home.

I woke up the next morning, my mouth dry and the sheets wrapped tightly around me in a jumbled mess. Clearly I had struggled in my sleep, and with no one to wake me as I thrashed around in the bed, the sheets and comforter had absorbed the beating. They looked spent.

The clock said nine fifteen. I was astonished I'd slept that long. Exhaustion has a way of warping time. I switched on my phone and saw there were three texts and five voice mails. Time to return to the real world of responsibility and accountability. The first text was from MarLea.

"Sorry you'll miss my game, Daddy. See you when you get home." It was hard to tell if it was a genuine regret or a guilt-inducing text born from Dayne's outrage. Either way, it deserved an answer. I texted back, "Love you, sweetie. See you when I get home tonight." MarLea rarely called me Daddy. Usually only when we were in my study listening to classical music, escaping. I felt a stab of guilt for leaving my daughter to handle her mother's frustration and anger toward me. If I really was a good guy, I

107

wouldn't have left my children in the midst of a firestorm. But how can you save kids if you're already suffocating yourself?

The next text was from Brooke. It was simple. "Tried to reach you this evening. Call when you can." I could call her on the drive back. I needed to shower and shave first. I needed food. I needed a moment of peace before I faced the reality of Carol's betrayal again.

The third text was easy. A promo offer. Deleted. Done.

I hit the voice mail button and listened to the messages. As expected the first two were from Dayne. She was practically screaming into the phone during the first message. "Mike, pick up the damn phone…Mike, I swear…you self-centered jerk…pick up the phone…" Then there was a click.

The second was eerily restrained. Three words in a steely voice. "Mike. Call me." It gave me goose bumps. It was too controlled, too restrained, almost pathologically detached. For the second time that morning, I felt true guilt for leaving my daughter behind. It took me a minute to hit the skip button. I saved the message. I'm not sure why.

The third message was from Rob. "Hey, Mike, I'm in the office looking over our current clients. I need to talk with you about the Henderson contract. Call me as soon as you can." No mention of Carol. Maybe our little firm would survive the crisis. Maybe Rob and I would figure it all out and move on. Just hearing Rob's voice mail gave me courage. I was incredibly relieved his message had been about business as usual and not about Carol.

The fourth and fifth messages were hang-ups. I checked my call log to see if I recognized the numbers and I didn't. I called Rob back.

"So where are you?" he asked after we'd handled the immediate business. "You're usually in by now."

"Yeah, I had to head north last night."

"You OK?"

"I am now. Just needed to get away for a while."

"Then I'll see you in the office later?"

"Yeah, I should be there in a few hours. Probably just after lunch." We talked a little more about the Henderson details before I hung up and started cleaning up.

Rob didn't have to ask why I didn't go home. He must have known things weren't good at my house. We'd been partners long enough. Women may talk in detail. A man's silence reveals more than words. Rob knew everything he needed to know about my home life by listening to my silence whenever he talked about Leanne and the way they'd conquered her cancer together. Dayne and I hadn't done anything of purpose together in so many years, I had nothing to share. My silence gave Rob all the information he needed.

As I showered, I realized the drive home was going to feel like walking the green mile to my own execution. I dreaded seeing the Getty on the hill, because it would be confirmation I was returning to an angry wife and a mess at work. Some men are greeted with a kiss at the door. I would be greeted with anger, but in order to see my children, I had to walk the gauntlet. The hard part for me was deciding who would walk through the door and face Dayne. Would it be Mike, the repentant husband who silently absorbed his punishment? Would it be Mike, the defensive businessman home from a long, difficult night on the road providing for his family? Or would it be the real Mike? I was beginning to wonder who the real Mike might be.

I stood in the shower, letting the warm water drip off my neck and roll down my back. If I wasn't a disappointing son, a clueless husband, a self-centered egotist, a pushover, a liar, a blind employer, an absent father…If I wasn't those things, who was I? Or more important, who was I going to be today, tomorrow, from now on? I began thinking about the traits I hated in my father, the traits I considered weak in my mother, the traits I admired in others. It's a dangerous game, this comparison shopping. I could always say I'm a better husband and father than my dad, a stronger spouse than my mother, a more devoted family man than my brother. But where did that leave me? Better than their greatest weaknesses. Small consolation.

I began to wish for a better measuring tool, a taller yardstick. I could hold myself up to other people's weaknesses and pale against their strengths, but ultimately it didn't matter. I only had to live with myself and decide for myself. If there is a God, and I probably needed to decide that question sooner rather than later, someday I might have to stand before him without the benefit of anyone else's cover or comparisons. As I looked out over the ocean, I realized it was time to decide who the real Mike Passick was and start being that man. It was time to stop allowing the actions of others to determine my fate, the attitudes of others to determine my actions. It was time to be myself. I just had to decide if that man was Dayne's husband and Carol's employer.

◄◆►

109

24

DECEMBER, SIXTEENTH YEAR

I grabbed a bagel and coffee from the hotel's breakfast bar, checked out, and began my drive south on the 101. Bits of fog hung near the coastal hills, wispy gray splotches against a backdrop of brown and green earth. A few open fields lay exposed to the morning sun, with an occasional worker's hat or tractor adding color to the brown rows of raised dirt. It was too beautiful a day for closed windows, so I opened my sunroof and let the air fill my car. It smelled of rich soil and salty air, a pleasant smell on a freeway. Certainly better than the clogged-freeway smells I usually encountered farther south. On the freeways of Southern California, my windows were perennially closed. Today as I drove the Central Coast they were blissfully open.

I scanned the radio, but it seemed distracting and irritating, like an insistent telemarketer. So I turned it off and drove with only the sound of the wind and the rich smells of the coastal air. Scents of sage, manure, trees, and ocean played inside my car like children in a park. They ran past my nose and, when they lost momentum, settled into cool, shady places around my feet. After all the drama, it was refreshingly peaceful. I needed to relax into this peace, because I knew it wouldn't last—it couldn't. I was driving back into the eye of the storm. Rob and I had to make a decision about Carol,

111

and I had to face Brooke once that decision was made. Then after all that, I would have the privilege of heading home to face my wife—Hurricane Dayne. She was sure to be a category four storm this time. I'd never hung up on her before or refused to return her calls for more than twelve hours. I would have to pay penance. The only question was how. The bigger question was whether I actually would. For the first time in my life, I felt little desire or compulsion.

I drove with my windows open to the sights and smells before the density of the Los Angeles basin overpowered them. My cell phone rang, and I checked to be sure it wasn't Dayne. Rob's voice was a welcome intrusion.

"Got a minute?"

"Sure. I'm just driving back. Should be there in a couple of hours."

As I expected, Rob responded without questions. "No problem. Just need your input on this client's situation."

Rob and I talked while I drove, and when we finished I thought about calling Dayne, but I didn't bother. I'd get home when I got there. Calling wouldn't make any difference in the outcome.

I expected to hit traffic as I entered L.A., but not so suddenly. Seventy miles an hour to zero is an abrupt change, and all around me, the faces of drivers reflected frustration and impatience. They had places to go. I didn't care when I arrived, and I can't quite explain how freeing that felt. It was an unaccustomed freedom to know it didn't matter for a few hours if I just sat quietly in my car. My mind wandered back to the bar, and I began second-guessing my decision to leave, so I switched on the radio just in time to hear a traffic report. A three-car accident on the 405 about four exits ahead. Serious injuries. I inched my way along for over an hour as four lanes of cars merged into one—the only lane we could drive on without disturbing the investigative evidence.

It was impossible not to see the covered body as I passed the scene. At least one fatality. Two ambulances were on site loading the injured. Two of the three cars looked horrible, a mass of crushed metal and broken pieces. Just as I passed, it struck me—the car nearest the covered body was the same as Dayne's. The same car she'd chosen two years ago to replace the SUV that replaced the minivan. A white BMW 5 Series. Suddenly the accident became personal.

For a long time, I couldn't think of anything but that white BMW. If that were Dayne driving, how would I have felt? Surprisingly, I felt sadness. I didn't want to hurt Dayne. I just wanted to stop the pain that kept masquerading as my marriage. The pain of knowing my wife didn't like me, that she had no desire to be married to me. The pain of her words about my inadequacies as a man, husband, and father. I thought about how my world would change if one of the ambulance victims was MarLea or Matt. My kids were important to me. So important I couldn't define myself fully without them. They were a part of my life that was irreplaceable.

"So who's important in your life?" I asked myself out loud. "Who else would you miss if you lost them?"

Carol. My mind shot the word out like a lightning bolt.

I'd miss my kids...and Carol. I'd miss my talks with Brooke. Those were the things I'd miss. And I might miss my job if somehow I couldn't practice law anymore. I liked many of my clients, and I liked being Rob's partner. We had a nice comfortable practice. I defined myself as a successful attorney. I would miss that. I would miss seeing Rob and Carol every day. They had become like family.

Suddenly, Brooke's offer sounded plausible. With some stipulations, some internal accountability, some preventative measures, maybe we could keep Carol. I didn't know if I could hold on to everyone I cared about, but maybe I could keep my kids and Carol.

113

25

DECEMBER, SIXTEENTH YEAR

Rob was bent over his desk working when I arrived at about two. He looked up when he heard my voice.

"So have you given more thought to Carol's situation?" I asked.

"Some."

"I've been thinking about it for the last couple of hours, once I stopped thinking about the accident."

"Was it a bad one?" Rob asked.

"Yeah. Looked like a fatality and some pretty serious injuries. One car was a white BMW like Dayne's."

"Oh," Rob said, looking up at me for a moment.

"A little too close to home."

Rob nodded.

"So, what do you think we should do about Carol?" I said, changing the subject.

"I'll be honest," Rob said. "I'd like to bring her back. Brooke's offer might be worth consideration since neither of us want to prosecute. I just think there have to be some consequences. Some things have to change."

"I agree," I said. "Maybe we can reduce her salary slightly and hand all the financial matters to a bookkeeper."

"That's a reasonable option, considering her only problem area was money."

"She's been a stellar receptionist. I honestly don't think we could find anyone our clients like more, or anyone who can answer their questions better," I said. "In fact, I think we may be doing ourselves and our clients a disservice to replace her in that role."

"But we have to limit her access to the money for a while," Rob said.

"I agree."

"Can we let her handle finances ever again?" he asked.

"I don't know. We'll have to see. For now, I think the answer is no."

"Agreed."

We talked for another hour, hammering out the details until we were both satisfied.

"So should we talk to Carol or Brooke or both?" I asked.

"Let's call Carol in, ask if she's OK with Brooke being part of the meeting, and if she is, we can get Brooke on the phone."

"That works," I said. "I'll call Carol."

At four thirty, Carol was sitting in my office and Brooke was on speakerphone.

"We've given this a lot of thought," Rob began. "And we've decided to reinstate you, Carol, with some conditions."

Carol sighed deeply and gave us both a tentative smile.

"First," he continued, "we will be reducing your salary by five hundred dollars a month. That will help us with the cost of a bookkeeper. Your job will no longer include handling the money."

"I understand," Carol said.

"Second," Rob continued, "Brooke has researched some counseling options, including a seminar on personal finance. Attending this seminar and six months of personal counseling are a mandatory part of your reinstatement." He paused for a moment and then continued. "We've checked and your medical insurance will cover the counseling."

Carol nodded. Brooke remained silent.

"Third, we will divide the remaining amount owed into three parts. Mike and I will write off eight thousand dollars. Brooke, you and Carol's

116

kids may pay off ten thousand dollars if your offer still stands. And Carol, we would like you to pay back five thousand dollars over two years, interest free. We can take it directly out of your paycheck if you wish."

There was silence for a few seconds, and then Brooke spoke.

"Aunt Carol, how do you feel about this offer?"

"I'd like to come back to work," Carol said. "And I'd like to take responsibility for at least some of what I owe you." She looked at both Rob and me. "It sounds like a very fair and generous offer...clearly more generous than I deserve."

Again, there was silence.

"I feel comfortable with everything I've heard," Brooke said. "I assume this agreement does not include any criminal prosecution."

"That's right," I said. "None of us want to see Carol with a criminal record. We all want her to learn to handle her personal finances and have the opportunity to remain with our firm."

"Good," Brooke said. "Thank you."

"Yes, thank you so much," Carol added, her eyes tearing up. "I'm so grateful."

"OK then," Rob said. "Carol, we'll have you sign a few papers, and then we'll see you tomorrow morning. Brooke, we'll send promissory note paperwork to you for your signature."

"I'll watch for it," Brooke said.

"Thanks, everybody. Hopefully this is the beginning of a better working relationship."

Carol hugged us both, then she left. Rob gathered his things and went home. I sat in my office and looked out the window. I needed to go home. It was the right thing to do. But I knew the outcome would not be nearly as clean or gracious as what Rob and I had just accomplished. Somehow I knew I just couldn't write off enough bad emotional debt to make my marriage work again. The debts were too high. The words lying in piles on the floor held too much weight and had become too heavy to remove.

26

DECEMBER, SIXTEENTH YEAR

I drove home the long way, past the restaurants and malls with their holiday displays, up the road past gated communities, and along parkways with beautifully decorated center dividers. All the holiday lights in the world couldn't improve my drive. I dreaded opening the front door.

MarLea was kicking a soccer ball around the driveway when I arrived.

"Hi, Dad." She grabbed the ball, walked over, and gave me a hug.

"Hi, kid. How's your mom?"

MarLea rolled her eyes and didn't say anything. She stood beside me as we both thought of something more to say.

"I played really well last night. I had an assist, and we won."

"Good for you, kiddo. I'm sorry I didn't get to see the game," I said.

"It's OK, Dad. You can come to the next one."

I made a mental note to be sure I did. *I need to put it on my calendar*, I thought. Maybe then I could actually show up on time. Make it a real appointment. I turned and walked toward the door. MarLea put her ball down and began kicking it again.

I opened the door to silence. Instead of calling, I just walked toward the kitchen. No one was there. MarLea's backpack was on the table, and Matt's jacket was in a pile on a chair. But the kitchen was empty. No dishes, no smells, no indication of life. I walked up the stairs to the bedrooms. Sounds were coming out of Matt's room. I stuck my head in. Matt was sitting at his desk, earbuds in, his foot tapping against the leg of the chair, a book open in his lap. I walked over and laid a hand on his shoulder.

"Hey, son."

"Hey, Dad."

"Studying hard?"

"Yeah, I have a test tomorrow."

"You'll do well."

"I hope."

I smiled. He smiled. Conversation over. Matt put his earbuds in and resumed tapping his foot. I turned and headed down the hall toward the master suite.

Dayne sat silently in a chair, her back to the door, looking out a window.

"I'm home," I said as I entered.

"I know," she said without turning.

"Do you want me to leave?" I asked, surprising even myself with the words.

"It's up to you," she replied, turning toward me. "It always is. You always do whatever you want without any regard for my feelings."

"Look, Dayne, I don't want to fight. If you want me to leave, I will. If you want to talk this out, I'll do that too. But I don't want to fight, and I don't want you to attack me."

"Don't worry," she said coldly. "I have no intention of attacking you. You've proven you'll just hang up on me."

"I'm sorry I hung up on you," I said truthfully. "It's been a hell of a week, and I just didn't have the energy to fight with you."

"I'm sure," she said flatly.

"So how do we navigate tonight, and tomorrow, and the rest of this week?" I asked.

Dayne stood and faced me. She had a determined, powerful look. It struck me as a look I might see from an opposing counsel. An "I will win" look.

"Here's the way I see it, Mike," she said with force, her voice rising with each syllable. "You have two options. Either you get some counseling and see if you can save this marriage, or we end it. I cannot—I will not—continue to live with a workaholic, selfish man who thinks only of money and never of his family. A man who won't return his wife's frantic calls or bother to show up for his kids' games. I'm sick to death of living with you, and either you get some counseling for your problems, or I'm done. Sometimes I wish I'd never married you. You're a pathetic husband and father. A selfish, selfish shell of a man. I'm through pretending you're not."

I stood there staring at the ghost of my father dressed as a woman. The ghost was yelling from above my head; the words burrowed painfully into my very soul. And suddenly I saw my mother dressed in my clothes, standing in my shoes, absorbing the verbal blows with her frail body. There were never any scars afterward. She never even acknowledged her pain. And I had become just like her. Hiding my pain, running from the reality of my life, wishing for something better but doing nothing to make it happen.

"You're right, Dayne," I said, pulling myself up to my full height. She looked at me with cynical eyes. "You're absolutely right about one thing. We need counseling. Not just for what you term 'my problems' but for the lousy way we've both shown up in this marriage." Dayne didn't stop me at that point, so I continued. "There's no doubt I've put work ahead of my family. I'm ready to change that. But there's also no doubt you have some things to change too. I'm willing to go to counseling if you are. If we're both prepared to face our own issues, we might be able to save this dysfunctional marriage."

Dayne stood perfectly still for what seemed like minutes. She didn't take her eyes off me. She stared at me with eyes of steel. Then she silently walked out of the room. I heard the garage door open and her car engine start. An hour later, I asked the kids if they'd eaten. They hadn't, so we drove to Chick-Fil-A and got takeout. I was surprised how easy it was to talk to my kids about their lives. We hadn't done that much recently.

It wasn't until later I realized two pairs of Dayne's shoes were missing from the closet and her makeup bag was gone. For some reason, I felt only relief as I crawled into bed alone that night.

121

27

DECEMBER, SIXTEENTH YEAR

The next day, when I arrived home from work, Dayne was making dinner. She didn't greet me, but there were four places set at the table. We managed a congenial dinner. Like well-mannered strangers, she and I passed the food and kept the conversation going. After dinner, I retreated to my study and she went to the bedroom.

An hour later, she stood at the door of my study.

"Mike, I'd like to try counseling."

"OK." I wanted to ask why she'd arrived at the conclusion after storming out of the house last night, spending the night at someone else's house. I decided to let the reason lie unspoken.

"My friend Rachel suggested a counselor. Do you have a preference?"

"No. I'm open to your friend's suggestion."

"OK. I'll call for an appointment. When are you available?"

"I'm pretty available any day after three or before ten. I can make that work in my schedule."

"Fine. I'll let you know."

If only all our conversations were this professional, I thought. I could handle this. It didn't feel intimate, but it didn't feel acrimonious either. I'd give up a little warmth for less anger. I'm not unreasonable.

The truth was, I wasn't unreasonable—I was completely and totally disengaged. The last thread of my commitment was frayed and barely holding. My desire to save our marriage was being kept alive by a respirator. I had nothing to lose by going to counseling. If a counselor had the surgical instruments to save our marriage, I was ready to lie on the table exposed. As long as Dayne would strip down too. I wasn't convinced she would, but I forced myself to have hope.

Dayne made our first appointment four weeks later, after the holiday rush had settled and the kids were back in school. The counselor, Stuart Boulton, was in his mid-fifties and had filled his office with plaid wingback chairs and a leather couch so it felt more like his personal library than a room for emotional evisceration. He was a strong-jawed, large-boned man who used to be on the golf team at Georgia Tech. Dr. Boulton had a fine mist of an accent that made his questions seem less intrusive, his advice less demanding. Truth was, he didn't demand anything of us. The first appointment went well, and both Dayne and I were willing to return. Dr. Boulton asked insightful questions, dug for the honest answers, and challenged us to become better human beings and partners. He met with us together at times and individually. I found myself looking forward to our conversations.

At the end of six months, I began to have some insight. I began to see why I worked obsessively, why I was satisfied with and comforted by Brooke's occasional phone calls, why I was content with a lack of intimacy in my marriage. I began to understand why I sold myself short over and over—in the back of my mind, I'd decided it was the best I could do. My role was the workhorse. Workhorses are housed in barns, they are fed the same grain day after day with an occasional apple once or twice a year, they are expected to perform, rarely praised, and often prodded. I had to change my view of myself and my view of life. In order to change my situation, I had to learn to be something besides a tired, overworked horse.

As much as I craved healing and changing, I watched Dayne fight it. The counselor pointedly asked her one day if she was afraid of losing control, and to my surprise, she burst into tears. They discussed the details in a private session, which neither shared with me, so I never fully understood why the word *control* had triggered Dayne that way. But our home life remained stalemated. Dayne wasn't berating and attacking me the way she once had, but she and I had forgotten how to connect, and six months of counseling didn't seem to be teaching us that vital marital skill. We lived in a state of detached parallel play—children on a playground engrossed in their own activity and desires, pretending to be friends when physical proximity demanded it.

28

SEVENTEENTH YEAR

For a while, counseling brought insights to the surface of my brain. I looked forward to the sessions because they helped me see ways I'd contributed to the sickness in my marriage. But in an odd juxtaposition, counseling had exposed how much Dayne blamed me for the dysfunction in our marriage and how little she was willing to reveal or deal with her part in our difficulties. At the beginning of counseling, I'd been willing to give up anything to save my marriage. Now, after nearly a year of sitting in the hot seat, I was ready for Dayne to take a turn.

It all came to a head in Dr. Boulton's office one Tuesday afternoon. We were discussing my long workday habits again, and I got frustrated.

"Look," I said directly to Dayne, "I'm more than willing to admit my role in our marital difficulties. I've already admitted I shouldn't be working such long hours, I should have spent more time at home focusing on the kids and on you, I've already admitted that. Can we move on to the things you're willing to admit?" Dr. Boulton straightened in his chair and looked directly at me.

"You sound frustrated," he said.

"I am."

"Why?"

"Because month after month, session after session, I sit here and admit my mistakes so we can dissect them. But it doesn't feel like my wife is willing to do the same."

Dr. Boulton looked at Dayne.

"Are you?" he asked her.

"Of course," Dayne said. But I heard the inflection in her voice. It was the same tone she used when she was lying to a friend about why we couldn't attend their dinner party. It was her stage voice. Practiced, cultivated to appear natural and calm. "I have nothing to hide," she continued. "If I've contributed in any way to our marriage issues, I'm more than willing to talk about it. But Mike has never told me I've been inadequate."

"Mike." Dr. Boulton turned to me. "Is there anything specific you'd like us to discuss?"

I sat there for a few moments, realizing I'd just made a mistake no good attorney should ever make. No matter what I said now, my words would appear accusatory, reactive, defensive, entirely wrong. I had just made a fool's mistake by initiating a discussion about Dayne. I should have let Dr. Boulton do that, but idiotically, I'd been too impatient.

"Dr. Boulton," I said, "I don't want to be the one to list my wife's shortcomings. I don't want to fight with her about what we view as each other's faults. I'd rather focus on learning and growth."

He nodded. Dayne looked out a window at two birds on a branch nearby. She crossed her legs away from my direction.

"Do you feel we've focused too much on your faults?" he asked.

"I'm not the professional counselor," I said. "I don't know the best way to heal a marriage. However, I do think both of us have a part to play in the healing."

"Of course," Dr. Boulton said. "So let me take a couple of sessions with each of you individually, and then we can schedule another time for the three of us to talk."

As we walked out of the office that day, the muscles in Dayne's face were tense. She strode to the car and opened her own door before I had a chance to get there. We drove home silently, but the minute I turned off the ignition in the garage, Dayne turned toward me in anger.

"What the hell was that?" she asked.

I didn't answer.

128

"We went to counseling to get a handle on your compulsive workaholism. We went to counseling so you could see how you're wrecking this family by being so self-centered and uncaring."

She paused for a breath.

"And you have the audacity to make it sound like we're both equally responsible for damaging this marriage. All I've ever done is care for the kids, keep the house, screw you even when I'm not in the mood, make sure I ran everything within our budget, and you have the *audacity* to suggest this is my fault!" She was screaming now. "You'll never get it. It's your fault we're in this mess. You are a terrible husband and an absentee father. So go ahead...give it your best shot at counseling. Throw me under the bus so you feel better about yourself. Maybe you'll find some magic way to make everything my fault. Good luck."

She opened the car door, stepped out, and slammed it behind her. The entire car shook. I sat in the driver's seat with one hand on the steering wheel and the other on the center console. Of course this was how the session would end. I'd made the mistake of openly suggesting she had done something wrong. My mistake...my very big mistake.

The next morning, I arrived at work, greeted Carol and Rob, and then closed my office door. It was a deliberate move. I wanted to hear Brooke's voice. I wanted to feel as if someone in the entire world cared to hear my voice. I wanted connection to someone who viewed me as an attractive man. Sometime the night before, between the time Dayne had slammed the car door and the time I'd walked a few miles in the dark then returned to sleep on the couch in my study, I'd stopped caring whether my relationship with Brooke was kosher or not. It was now a matter of survival. I needed to hear a voice that wasn't continually angry or disappointed with me. That morning, it felt as though I would drown in despair if I didn't hear Brooke's voice, so I picked up the phone and dialed her number.

"Hi, Mike," Brooke said immediately. "I was just thinking about you."

"I hope that's good," I said.

"Always," she replied. "Thoughts of you are always good."

"Brooke, do you have a few minutes to talk?"

"Sure. Do I need to close my office door?"

"Yeah. If you don't mind."

There's a place inside a man where hopes and aspirations live. It's right next door to the vulnerable place of fear. For the next hour, I gave Brooke a guided tour of those hidden places, and she quietly listened. I shared the truth about my marriage...not just the whitewashed version of a marriage in decline, but the raw wounded version of accusation, anger, and disconnection. Whenever I faltered, Brooke asked a question or verbally took my hand and allowed me to keep walking down a path I'd avoided for over sixteen years. When I finally finished, I sat quietly in my chair, staring at my diplomas on the wall and the pictures on my desk. I was completely exhausted. It took Brooke a few seconds to realize I was done.

"Mike, are you all right? That was tough stuff."

"Yeah, I'm OK. I'm just tired."

"Do you mind if I ask you something?"

"No, go ahead."

"How long has she been telling you you're lazy and selfish?" Brooke asked.

"Since early...since the kids were little. Maybe before."

She was quiet for a moment. Then she gently asked, "Are you?"

"Am I lazy or selfish?"

"Yes."

"I don't know," I said. "How do any of us know for sure? How do I really, truthfully know if I work such long hours for my family's benefit or for my own ego? How do I know..." My words trailed off into a blur of self-doubt. Then I continued. "I think that's the very hardest part about listening to Dayne's accusations week after week, year after year...I can't tell whether they're true or not."

All I heard was silence for a while. Brooke took a deep breath and exhaled slowly.

"Wow, Mike," she said. "You're making me rethink every word I ever said to my husband...every argument we ever had."

"Why?" I asked.

"Because I realize it's easy to say things that are partially true and partially false. Things that tear holes in the fabric of another person's self-worth and self-belief. And now I see what they do, the damage they cause. Maybe those are the cruelest type of accusations—how is the other person supposed to tell where the truth begins and ends?"

I thought for a moment. So many times I'd been overwhelmingly confused by Dayne's indictments. I viscerally knew they weren't totally true, but I didn't have the tools to pull the thread of truth out of the tightly woven fabric that surrounded it. Instead I absorbed it all and the words smothered me. After years I had become, in my core, confused and uncertain of the truth about me.

"Brooke," I said, "I don't know what to believe anymore...about myself or about my marriage."

"I have no words of wisdom about your marriage," she said softly. "All I can do is listen and hope that helps you. But Mike...I do have some wisdom about you."

She paused, probably to listen for my reaction, but I was too tired to make a sound.

"I know you are a man of compassion and strength. I know you're a good man who has overcome difficult circumstances and held to his values when he could have run away from both. I know you love your kids and are committed to your marriage. Those things are the truth. I know it."

"If you know that as truth, why doesn't my wife?" I asked.

The phone went silent again. "I can't speak for Dayne," Brooke said. "I can only speak from my perspective. The Mike I know is all of those good things and more. You're a good man, Mike. I know that. And I haven't seen laziness or selfishness in you yet."

"Thanks, Brooke," I said. "That means a lot to me. You're a great friend. Thanks."

"Mike," she said, "please don't give up. Things are hard right now, but it's going to get better."

"I can only hope."

After I hung up the phone, I sat for a few minutes before I got up and opened the door. How, I wondered, was I supposed to love a woman who despised and accused me, and not love a woman who admired and enjoyed me? How was I supposed to stay faithful to my wife and not share myself fully with Brooke? My feelings for Brooke were growing deeper and stronger, and my feelings for Dayne were fading like the last rays at dusk.

Somehow I managed to make it through the day, gather my things, start my car, and drive home to my family. I walked into the house to find a wife whose anger had receded. Dinner was on the table, and she'd rented a movie for us to watch together.

Maybe it wasn't so bad after all. Maybe all I needed to do was talk with Brooke and drive home to my family. Maybe that was the practical compromise it would take to survive.

29

JULY, EIGHTEENTH YEAR

Rob and I had made the right decision about Carol. She and Brooke both made regular payments and finally repaid our firm $15,000. Brooke came out to California periodically to visit, and we often had lunch at a little restaurant in Laguna Beach. I'd be lying if I said our relationship was completely platonic. It wasn't. But it wasn't a torrid affair either. I had my limits and she had hers. We recognized the chemistry, and for the most part we stayed away from adultery in the technical sense, although I was very aware that I felt more emotional connection with her than with Dayne. It was hard to draw a physical line when my mind and body wanted more, but somehow we held that line. Deep within me, I wondered if Dayne had created a connection outside our marriage too. She shopped, had lunch with friends regularly, and went to the gym. She talked at times about men at the gym or friends' husbands or fathers of our kids' schoolmates. But she never opened the conversation wide enough for me to see inside, to look for clues of an affair or an attachment. In truth, I didn't want to know. It was easier to avoid the subject than open my own life to scrutiny. I was comfortable here, living as Dayne's husband and Brooke's friend. But somehow I knew it couldn't last.

"I'm dating someone," Brooke told me one day in July as we sat overlooking the water in Laguna. She was in California on business again. I felt as if I'd been stabbed.

133

"Are you OK?" Brooke asked, her hand gently touching my arm. "I didn't mean to drop that on you."

"Of course I'm OK," I said quickly. "I'm glad to hear you're dating again. It's been a year or two since your divorce, hasn't it?"

"Just over two," she answered.

"So what's he like? How'd you meet?" I tried to sound interested... happy for her. I wasn't either.

"We met through a mutual friend. Steve is really nice. He owns his own insurance agency and has been a widower for a couple of years."

"Is he old?"

Brooke laughed. "No. His wife died of cancer in her early forties. He's two years older than I am."

"Kids?"

"No. They didn't try until their late thirties, and when they decided to start fertility treatments, the doctors discovered her cancer."

"Oh," I said. "That's sad."

"It is. Steve's a really nice man."

"Nicer than me?" I asked, wishing I hadn't the moment the words hit the table.

"Come on, Mike," Brooke said, shaking her head. "I'm not dumb enough to believe we have anything more than friendship with chemistry. You've had ample time to end your marriage if you wanted to be with me."

"You never asked me to end it."

"I never would," she said emphatically. "That's not my call. It's yours. You and your wife have been in counseling. That told me you were trying to save things, not end them."

I gazed out over the ocean. Who knew? I had no idea Brooke viewed me as marriage material. The question was: Did I want to do anything about it now?

"So you think this guy could be the one?" I asked, filled with curiosity.

"I don't know. I wouldn't keep dating him if there was no chance at all."

I went back to my chicken. Brooke leaned back in her chair.

"Look, Mike," she said. "I like you a lot. We have plenty of attraction going on, and we've proven our friendship can outlast difficulty. But I believe in my heart you want to stay married—to keep your family together, even at the expense of your own happiness. You're that kind of guy." She reached over and placed her hand over mine. "I admire you more than you know. I think you're a wonderful man. But I will not be the woman who encourages you to leave your wife and children. You can't do that right now. You're too invested and you're too honorable. It would destroy the friendship we have."

She was right. I hated it, but she was right.

After I dropped Brooke off at her hotel, I drove back to the office with the windows open. So what if the smells of Southern California freeways couldn't match the smells of the Central Coast. I had chosen to live here, and I would relish the smells of my choice.

While I still claimed Brooke as a friend, I realized I needed to stop calling her. I didn't know Steve, but I knew men. No guy wants another man calling his girlfriend regularly. I wouldn't want some guy doing that to me, so I afforded Steve the same respect. Brooke called me once when she came to California, but neither of us pushed the issue of talking in person. The phone was enough, and after a while even that seemed wrong, so I stopped calling. It's impossible to explain how empty and lonely I felt for weeks after, but the best way is to say it felt like wandering back into the desert after splashing and playing in a cool stream.

30

OCTOBER, NINETEENTH ANNIVERSARY

I tried to think of an appropriate way to celebrate our nineteenth anniversary. After one year of regular counseling and two years of periodic help sessions, Dayne and I had reached a plateau. She still berated me occasionally, and I still took it, watching bit by bit as the last remnants of my love for her sank into the Pacific. Our kids were both teenagers, so we found ourselves alone in the house more often, and instead of finding a renewed passion, we often went our separate ways for the evening. I longed for something, so I joined a gym, began writing a legal thriller, and played golf more frequently and more seriously. It didn't fill the void, but it provided distraction.

Five weeks before our nineteenth anniversary, I broached the subject.

"Want to get away to Palm Springs or head to Hawaii for our anniversary?" I asked Dayne one evening after dinner. MarLea had just left for a study session at a friend's house. "I found a nice resort in Palm Springs and a lovely hotel on Maui. Both are available the week of our anniversary."

"That's OK," Dayne replied absentmindedly.

"Does that mean yes or no?" I asked, trying to clarify her answer.

137

"No," she said. "I really don't want to go anywhere." She had her back to me as she unloaded dishes from the dishwasher.

"OK," I said. I got up from the table and walked into my study. I turned on Beethoven. It was rich and full and brilliant—instruments working together to produce an incredible sound. No one on this CD was indifferent. Each musician was engaged, playing his or her best. Playing the correct notes in the correct time, following the conductor's baton.

I was sick of listening to the sounds of my marriage. Dayne and I were playing from two different scores. Although we appeared to be following the conductor's baton, attentive to our counselor as he guided us through each session, we could never make music. All we did was create dissonance where there should have been harmony.

"It's hopeless," I said out loud. "I give up."

I put my head in my hands, leaned my elbows on the table, and officially gave up. I'll never forget that day. It was the day I buried my hopes, the day I realized I was trying to revive a corpse. My marriage wasn't hopeless—it was dead. The gangrene had spread into the soul of my marriage, and trying to resuscitate it was a waste of energy.

I lay in bed that night staring at the ceiling. Dayne's breathing was regular and shallow. She was lying on her side, her back to me, cuddling a pillow tightly. I looked at her. Would I miss her if we divorced? Did I have the courage to make a different life for myself, to face aloneness in some bachelor apartment? Did I have the fortitude to face my children and tell them I was leaving their mother? There was no need for me to worry. I didn't have to do any of that. Three days after our anniversary—three days after we let our anniversary pass with nothing more than a mention and two impersonal cards with only our names signed—Dayne met me at the door when I arrived home after work on Monday. She hadn't done that in years, so I knew something was wrong.

"Mike," she said without hesitation, "I'm leaving."

"OK," I said, unaware. "When will you be back?"

"I'm not coming back," she said. "I'm moving in with Ted Conner."

The right hook hit my jaw, and the pain spread through my face.

"He and I have been seeing each other for a while, and we have something you and I never had. I can't stay in this marriage any longer. You're not the man I want." She didn't even stop for a breath as the words came flooding out. "Ted's left his wife, and I'm leaving you."

"OK," I said. I didn't know what to say. I've never been quick on my feet after a blow to the head.

"I would have told you months ago," Dayne said matter-of-factly. "I never wanted another anniversary to go by, but Ted had to find the right time to tell his wife. So that's why I'm telling you now."

"Oh." I couldn't speak more than one syllable. It took everything to get that out of my mouth.

"I hope we can divide things amicably and not let this affect our role as parents to Matt and MarLea," she continued. "I'm sure our counselor can help us figure those things out." Her voice was steady, certain.

"You want to keep going to counseling?" I asked, confused.

"I think it would be a good idea. He can help us figure out how to be joint-custody parents for the next few years until the kids are on their own."

"OK," I said.

"Mike, you need to understand I'm leaving you. You aren't the husband I want or need. You never have been. I'm not even sure I ever loved you."

I stood silent.

"Counseling hasn't seemed to help you much. You're still ridiculously self-centered. I hope you can find a way to get over yourself, to think of someone besides yourself and money. Hopefully someday you can find some happiness with someone else," she said as she lifted a suitcase and began walking toward her car. "I've decided to do that for myself. Hopefully you can too.

"By the way," she added as she opened the car door. "MarLea is at Catherine's for the next two days. She'll be back on Wednesday afternoon. She'll probably move in with me soon, so you don't have to worry about learning her schedule. I doubt she'll want to be with you any more than I do."

I watched her drive away, her car piled with boxes I hadn't noticed before. I walked into the house and stopped in front of the painting over the fireplace. That red dress once spoke to me of passion, the red lips whispered desire. Those hands once touched me and explored my body. Those children were born of a love that existed once a very long time ago. But that family didn't exist anymore. I wondered if it ever truly had.

◈

139

31

THE YEAR

The counselor urged us to try a bit longer, to use a different approach, to excavate hope from the ruins. But Dayne was done. She refused to hear anything except ways to help our kids cope with their parents' divorce. In fact, she looked radiant and happy when she came to the sessions. I looked sad and rejected. Clearly Ted was offering something I never provided. Dayne's smiles were clear indicators of my inadequacies, my faults, and my rotten attempts at being a husband. I came away from the two sessions with a clear understanding of how to support my kids through a divorce and how to keep from using them as pawns in the division of our larger chessboard. But I learned very little about how to stand in a room with a wife who was sleeping with MarLea's friend's father and pretend it was all fine. I never mastered that skill. I spent a lot of time at those sessions avoiding eye contact with Dayne. I didn't want to see her happy with Ted. I just wanted to go back to the office and work.

It's a funny thing about memory. During those counseling sessions, I tried to remember the little things, thinking maybe they would be cathartic and I could begin the process of healing. But I realized something. I couldn't remember the in-between things, the little details of those nineteen years I spent married to Dayne. Believe me, I tried.

I wanted to remember the normal conversations about kids' teachers or car purchases or Christmas gifts. But I couldn't. Maybe it was the suddenness of Dayne's departure, maybe it was the realization that most of our marriage had been spent apart, either sleeping without touching or working without communicating. Whatever the reason, most of the day-to-day had been subtly erased from my memory. I remembered the highs, a beautiful bride walking down the aisle and taking my arm, the birth of our children, and the lows, the worst of Dayne's accusations, the weeks without touching. But I'd forgotten the things that would have brought me comfort; the little details that would have helped me remember our life together. Sometimes, for a brief moment, my memory gave me a glimpse of Dayne in bed reading, and I remembered she read regularly before turning off the light to sleep, her hair falling over her eyes and her hand reaching up to brush it away. I could capture a brief memory of walks in the neighborhood, Dayne and I holding hands and walking in perfect cadence as our small children ran ahead to chase a cat or point out a caterpillar on the sidewalk. It made me sad that I could not remember more.

I thought if I sat quietly, memories might come back, but I couldn't bear to sit quietly and think—I couldn't bear it for years after Dayne left. The memories that came back weren't comforting. They were sad or painful or ego destroying. So I went back to the only thing that had ever allowed me to avoid painful thoughts—work. It was a full year before I even considered I might find solace in golf, or friends, or travel. At first, it was just me and work, with periodic guest appearances by MarLea and Matt. Now I know why presidents and prime ministers keep diaries. History would be lost if you left it to periodic recollection, to someone like me attempting to remember nineteen years in one document. Only the discipline of daily recording makes it possible to analyze history the way historians must.

I do remember this: within days of Dayne's leaving, MarLea started slipping into the depression that marked her entire fourteenth year. She had been as surprised as I was when two sets of parents from her class became one couple with two leftover, discarded spouses. Dayne and Ted had managed to keep their affair a secret from everyone until the moment when Ted told his wife and Dayne told me in a perfectly choreographed tango of escape. Ted's wife never reached out to me, and I had no reason to call her, but our daughters were friends and had been classmates since first grade. They were devastated.

I'll never forget that Wednesday when MarLea arrived home. I had assumed Dayne would tell her. After all, Dayne was the one who made this

142

choice. It was her job to convey the news. But I was wrong. Dayne left it to me to inform the kids. I was working in my study when MarLea arrived that Wednesday, backpack slung across one shoulder.

"Hey, Dad. You working from home today?"

I looked at her and nodded.

"Where's Mom?"

I looked into MarLea's face and realized suddenly she had no idea. She was about to be hit with the emotional right hook of her life, and she didn't even have her hands up in a protective stance. It was going to smack her full face, and I couldn't think of a single way to protect her.

"Maybe you better call her," I said.

"Something wrong?"

"Maybe you should call her."

"Dad, tell me," she said. "Is Mom all right? Did something happen to her?" The words flew out of MarLea's mouth like buckshot.

"Dad." Her voice was insistent now. "Tell me."

I searched for the right words, but my hesitation just agitated her more.

"Tell me, Dad."

"Your mom left." I regretted saying anything the moment the words were out. Would Dayne berate me for being too harsh? Would MarLea remember this moment as the time her dad failed her? She dropped into the nearest chair and let her backpack fall to the ground. Her eyes never left my face.

"Left? Like left for a couple of days or left for forever?"

"Yes."

"Which one? Forever?"

"Yes."

"Oh." Her eyes dropped to the floor.

"Maybe you should call her," I suggested again.

"Yeah," MarLea said quietly. After a pause, she added, "Clearly, she didn't think it was that important to call me."

"She probably didn't want to mess up your time with friends," I said.

"Yeah...probably."

MarLea picked up her backpack and turned to walk out of the room. She paused in the doorway and then turned back to face me.

"Does Matt know?"

"I haven't told him."

"OK," MarLea said quietly. "I will."

I sat in my study in silence for some time. Beethoven, Chopin, and Rachmaninoff held no appeal. I wondered if I should go upstairs and try to comfort MarLea or explain to Matt, but I was running on empty myself, so I just sat in silence until the light through the window faded and the room became darker than my thoughts. I got up slowly and walked toward the kitchen, listening to the sounds of Beyoncé coming from MarLea's room. Instead of trying to coax food out of the kitchen, I walked slowly up the stairs and knocked on MarLea's door.

"Yeah," she said through the closed door.

"Hey, you want to get some food?"

The door opened.

"Sure, Dad," she said softly. Her eyes were red, and traces of mascara added darkness under her lower lids. I had expected anger. Instead I saw vulnerability and pain. She looked like I felt. Clearly the right hook had hit hard. The anger might come later, but right now it just looked as if my daughter needed a hug. I reached over and put my arm around her. She leaned into my chest and began sobbing.

"I knew it," she said. "I knew Mom would leave."

"I'm so sorry, honey," I said softly.

"It's OK, Dad," she said. And then she uttered the words I have held in my heart ever since. The words that told me it might not be entirely my fault and gave me a glimmer of hope in the depths of darkness, a sliver of light shining down into a collapsed mine shaft. "Mom was never happy here anyway. She was always upset. I knew she would leave eventually."

I held MarLea in my arms for a few more minutes. She cried and then she wiped her eyes on the back of her hand and looked up at me.

"Come on, Dad," she said. "Let's go get Matt and get some food. Maybe I'll call Mom later."

144

32

THE YEAR

MarLea called Dayne two days later. For some reason, she needed to find the courage to dial her mom's number, and when she did find that courage, she was shocked to hear her mother so happy. I didn't hear the conversation, because I was at work. But MarLea told me that evening.

"Mom sounded really happy," MarLea said. She looked confused and hurt. "She said she misses Matt and me, and we can come over anytime. She made it sound like we could just pop over for a visit. But she didn't actually invite me."

I didn't say anything. I just kept making the chicken tacos we'd agreed on for dinner. It was one of the few things I could make for my kids.

"Do you think Mom is happy with Mr. Conner?" MarLea asked. "Do you think it will work out for them?"

I looked at my daughter, trying to figure out how to say I had no idea without sounding flippant or rude. So instead of answering her, I used an old trick and redirected the question.

"Honey," I said, "long-term relationships are a big step in the best of circumstances. I don't think this situation qualifies as the best of circumstances."

"No, it doesn't," MarLea said. She got up from the bar stool she was sitting on, walked over to a kitchen drawer, and pulled out three placemats. "Is Matt coming home for dinner?"

145

"I think so," I said.

"Then I'll set a place for him."

"Thanks."

I put shredded cheese in a bowl. Maybe the next night we'd just go out. Either that or I needed to learn how to make something besides nachos, quesadillas, and tacos, the staples of my bachelor life.

"Dad, Mom's not coming back, is she?"

"I don't think so," I said. I wanted to be more positive for my daughter, to give her hope that Dayne and I might reconcile. But I already knew the marriage was over. Ted had already given Dayne something I hadn't been able to provide in almost two decades—happiness. Why would she want to return to me?

Matt, MarLea, and I ate dinner together with the TV on. No one really wanted to talk. I had no wisdom to share, and they seemed to need distraction from the reality that three of us were eating at a table that used to seat four. Both kids helped me clear the table and load the dishwasher, and then they wandered to their own rooms to do homework.

"Thanks for dinner, Dad," Matt said. "At this rate we won't starve."

I smiled. At least Matt and MarLea knew I was trying. At least I wasn't a complete failure as a husband and father. Well, maybe as a husband, but one out of two was the best I could do under the circumstances.

I walked into my study hoping to find a pressing deadline to force my attention away from the pictures of our family scattered across my desk and bookcase. Dayne at the beach with small children at her feet playing in the sand. A picture of Dayne and me at a fundraiser, my arm around her shoulders. I hated seeing them, but I wasn't ready to remove them either. That seemed too rude and final.

How was it possible that I once loved Dayne so completely that the thought of life without her seemed inconceivable? This complex woman who developed the skills to shred my confidence and disembowel my view of success was the same woman who had promised to love and cherish me until death do us part.

I searched for a contract that needed review. Instead, in an old stack of to-be-filed papers, I found a parking stub from one of Brooke's visits. I thought for a moment about calling her, about telling her that I was alone now and my wife would be crawling into bed tonight with Ted Conner. I thought about words I might use to explain the situation to Brooke in a way that didn't make me seem pathetic, victimized, or rejected. No words came immediately to mind, because in fact, I had been rejected. It seemed ludicrous to tell her something that would diminish my masculinity in her mind. I decided to avoid that phone call. Brooke would probably ask questions and I was a little short on answers at the moment. Plus I realized suddenly—I couldn't call Brooke. I was alone but she wasn't. She'd told me a while back that she was seeing Steve, and I'd heard no news of a breakup. My mind circled in on that fact like a bull's-eye. She was taken. Brooke wasn't there for me anymore. Someone else now claimed her attention and had every right to it.

Of all the times in my life when I've felt alone, that moment of realization was probably the most painful. I understood with stabbing clarity that while I was trying to hold back my feelings for Brooke, while I was trying to keep from having a full-on affair, my wife had been cultivating her exit strategy and probably screwing Ted. I'd been stupid. I had passed up the opportunity to have Brooke for myself, and now someone else had her and was never going to let her go. Of course he wouldn't let her go...she was beautiful, intelligent, and enjoyable. I slumped down in my desk chair and ran my hands through my hair. Music couldn't reach me tonight. I didn't even try to find comfort with Mozart or Eliane Elias. I sat in dark solitary confinement and wondered if I would survive to ever see sunlight again. It took hours before I found the strength to walk upstairs and crawl into my ice-cold bed.

People throw around the phrase "Out with the old—in with the new." It's a harmless phrase until you realize you're the old. Dayne had defined me once again. I was the old. Ted was the new. And in my mind that night, I was old and stupid.

147

33

THE YEAR

I kept going to counseling after Dayne left, mainly because I needed someone to help me keep my frustration in check and because I knew the kids wouldn't consider counseling unless one of their parents did. Matt went a few times, but found his best therapy was the outdoors. He would run or bike or swim, and when I saw him, he appeared to be coping. MarLea, however, wasn't doing as well. She needed counseling to deal with the depression that hit her like tidal waves at the most unexpected times. I had no skills to help her. The logic that served me so well in business negotiations failed miserably with a teenage daughter, so it seemed all I had to offer was time together in the study and hugs when she cried. I held my daughter as she cried so many times during that year—her tears dripping through the sleeve of my shirt and penetrating my very soul. There were days I thought I would drown in MarLea's tears. Yet mine wouldn't come out. They stayed locked inside me as I absorbed more and more of MarLea's pain. I went to counseling because I needed to keep from shutting down entirely. I was facing the finality of a divorce, my daughter's surging hormones and depressive episodes, the distancing of my son, and the realization that another man was making my former wife very happy. Whether or not Dayne was actually blissful could be debated, but it certainly looked that way from the outside.

149

One day during that year of pure hell, Rob invited me to church. Rob had never been much of a Bible-thumper. I knew he and Leanne went to church, but I'd never been particularly interested in which one or, frankly, not all that interested in church period. But I was facing a life that seemed devoid of answers. My mind kept recycling the word *why*, and I kept realizing I had no responses—no answers for why my marriage had failed almost from the moment we met and no answers to the bigger questions of my life. Was I a good man? A decent father? Someone with a future? What was I supposed to do now?

I've heard people say church and religion are for the weak. Perhaps that's true. I certainly reached for it when I was exceptionally weak. Rob saw I'd lost my footing, and instead of preaching to me or handing me a pamphlet on theology, he just asked if I'd like to come to church and then lunch with him and Leanne. I said yes because I knew the house would be empty that weekend. MarLea was staying over at a friend's house.

Church didn't change my life that day. I didn't have an epiphany and definitely didn't hear voices from the sky calling my name. But as I watched Rob greet his friends and introduce me to them, it made me realize I didn't have many male friends. In fact, I didn't have much of a personal life at all, except with the recorded musicians in my study. I defined myself not as a fellow man among men, but as a dad, an attorney, an ex-husband. Somehow my life had excluded other guys, which was puzzling to me because I had lots of friends before Dayne and I married. I played sports. I watched games with other guys. We worked on cars together. Where had that camaraderie gone? I thought about that a lot as I drove to Rob and Leanne's house for lunch. I brought up the subject as soon as we began eating.

"So tell me about the guys you introduced me to as we walked in. Seem like nice guys."

Rob smiled. "Those are some of the guys in my small group."

"Small group?"

"Yeah."

"Like a Bible study?"

"Yeah, it's billed as that, but it's more like an accountability group," Rob said.

"So who comes?"

"Let's see," Rob said. "Tom, one of the guys you met this morning, is a high school football coach. Laurence owns a plumbing company and flies experimental aircraft he builds himself. Hank, the other guy you met, is a stockbroker who invests in commercial real estate. Jon is an orthopedic surgeon who specializes in hands. I round out the group, the attorney who gets the brunt of all the lawyer jokes."

"So do you sit in a circle and share your inner feelings?" I teased.

"Of course," Rob said with more than a hint of sarcasm. "You can see me doing that, can't you?"

I couldn't.

"So what do you guys do?"

"We get together once a week. We study sections of the Bible and talk about those, which usually leads to deeper discussions about what it means to be a husband, a father, a man...if we're living the values we believe."

"Sounds like baring the soul."

"Only if you want to."

"So you don't go around the room and expect an answer from everyone?"

"Hasn't happened that way yet," Rob said.

As we passed the food, the conversation flowed easily from Rob's small group to work to updates on our kids. When Leanne finished her last bite, we took our plates to the kitchen and dished up three servings of an amazing chocolate mint pie.

I thought about the idea of a men's group as I drove home. I wasn't convinced I would like church, and it seemed somewhat unnatural to have a group of men talk too deeply about anything but business. I already had a counselor. I didn't need more counseling. But the idea of talking with other men and getting their perspective had a certain appeal, and a group at church sounded like a better idea than guys in a bar. Seeing Rob's enthusiasm about his men's group had put a serious dent in my preconceived notion about church groups. I thought they were groups of older women or young mothers; groups designed to help women. I'd never considered the idea that churches could help men connect.

Maybe I could use the perspective of other men to navigate being the single parent of two teenagers. Dayne had demanded fifty-fifty custody, but in reality, the kids lived at my house and rarely spent the night anywhere else. They saw their mother at games and events, on holidays, and at their convenience. After all, they were teenagers, and they had other priorities. So did Dayne. She was busy living the life of Ted's pampered lover. By default, I became the majority-interest parent, and I was surprised to find my kids and I did pretty well at home when MarLea wasn't depressed. But I was in uncharted waters. I might need some good friends in my life to become the man I truly wanted to be. Maybe when I was ready I'd consider it, just as Rob had. For the moment, Dr. Boulton and our once-a-month counseling gave me a safe, familiar male perspective. His office had become a place of healing for me. I remember one particular appointment with him, when he invited me to call him Stuart. It must have been about six months after Dayne left—about the time I started referring to my life as BDL (Before Dayne Left) and ADL (self-explanatory). Stuart let me get away with that for a long time.

"So what's going to motivate you to keep getting up in the morning?" Stuart asked.

"Same thing as always. Work."

"Why? You don't have a wife to support anymore."

"I still have kids."

"Are your kids the reason you feel good about getting out of bed every morning?"

"I don't feel good about that or anything really. I just do it because it has to be done."

"I thought we decided you weren't going to be a workhorse anymore," Stuart said. "You didn't want to live for work alone. You made that statement months ago."

"You're right," I said. "I did decide that, but I don't have any idea how to implement it. I'm starting to feel brief flickers of enjoyment when I bike or golf or when I write. There are moments of connection with my kids that make me glad to be with them. But none of those are motivators to work this hard."

"So why are you working so hard, Mike?"

"I don't know."

I sat there realizing I really didn't know. I didn't care if I had the big house. I wanted to provide a college education for my kids, but I didn't have to work sixty hours a week to do that.

"I honestly don't know why I work this hard," I said.

"Maybe you're still trying to prove your worth to someone," Stuart said.

"What makes you say that?"

"Just a theory."

I thought for a moment. My father was dead. What would make me want to prove anything to him? My wife had left me. Why would I want to prove anything to her?

"Maybe I'm trying to prove something to myself," I finally said.

"Maybe..."

Suddenly my mind took the baton and began running with it. "Maybe," I said, "I'm trying to prove to myself that the accusations against me aren't true—that I'm not lazy or dumb or selfish."

Stuart looked directly at me before he spoke.

"Mike," he said, "you can never work hard enough to disprove those adjectives. You'll work yourself into the ground trying to disprove something that's already untrue. Before you leave today, I want to determine once and for all if you are or you are not any of those descriptors." He paused for emphasis. "So, Mike..." He turned his body toward me and looked directly into my eyes. "Are you a lazy man?"

I didn't answer. I just sat there looking at the flecks of gray and brown in the carpet. The carpet pile was about a quarter of an inch, and the flecks were randomly spaced. It was an unusual carpet pattern, one I suddenly found fascinating.

"Mike," Stuart repeated firmly but gently. "Are you lazy?"

"I don't know," I said. "I don't think so, but I can't be sure."

"Then answer this question," Stuart said. "Have you ever known anyone who was lazy?"

"Sure," I said. "A guy in college, one of my roommates."

"How did you determine he was lazy?"

"He didn't show up to class, he lay around all day smoking dope and watching TV, he wouldn't get a job until his parents threatened to cut him off."

"How do you know he wasn't depressed or addicted?" Stuart asked.

"You mean as opposed to lazy?"

"Yes."

"I don't. I'm just telling you at the time I thought he was lazy."

"So do you fit that mold?"

153

I sat staring at the carpet again. Did I fit that mold? Did I not show up?

"Look, Stuart, I get where you're going with this. No, in my mind I don't fit the mold of lazy or dumb or selfish. But what does it matter whether I think that or not? Other people clearly think that of me. I'm sure everyone thinks they're fine and normal. What matters to me is the way I'm perceived by the people I love."

"It is important how others view you," Stuart said. "As long as their view of you is coming from a healthy perspective. Mike, I never knew your dad, and I can't breech patient confidentiality to reveal things about your wife's emotional state, but I can tell you with absolute certainty that when you consider the judgments of other people about your character, you need to deeply discount the words of these two individuals. Their words do not come from a place of emotional health.

"You need to think about the man you want to be and see how you measure up to him. You need to surround yourself with healthy friends and consider their views. If you really want to judge what kind of man you are, use a decent evaluation tool. I can offer you some self-evaluative tools if you want, but I think you'll find you already have a number of good people who are already telling you everything you need to know."

"Already telling me?"

"How long have you been in practice with Rob?" Stuart asked.

"Sixteen or seventeen years I think."

"Has Rob ever once said, even hinted, you're lazy or selfish?"

"No."

"He ought to know. His business success is directly tied to your work ethic and your ability to be an unselfish partner. As much as anyone, Rob is telling you every day that you're a good man. If you're going to judge yourself, be sure the mirror you're looking into isn't flawed."

I thought about that for a long time after I left Stuart's office. I began to think about reflected judgments. Were my father's outbursts a reflection of my mother's actions or his own clouded view of the world? Were Dayne's accusations a reflection of me or a fogged view of her own unrealized expectations?

There was no doubt in my mind I could have worked less and been with my kids more, but it would have been impossible to provide the lifestyle Dayne expected and, frankly, demanded. If I'd worked less, I'd have been branded even lazier. If I worked more, I'd have been an even more selfish father. For the first time, I realized I had been locked in an impossible situation. The happiness I longed to give Dayne was unachievable because there was no path to a successful outcome. The only way I could have provided the lifestyle she longed for without working sixty-hour weeks was to be a trust-fund baby. I was born into the wrong family for that. In fact, I was born into the wrong family to ever please my father. He couldn't ever find a path to contentment either because his expectations could never be met by a human wife or either of his human sons. He wanted perfection and we could never be perfect. No amount of work would achieve the goals these two people wanted from me, and here I'd been working all my life to reach them.

By the time I reached home, I was mentally tired, but somehow energized. I had buried my father years ago, and I'd watched my wife walk out. Now I needed to remove the coiled snakes they had left around my neck. I walked up the front steps and shook their judgments of me onto the porch. Like serpents that had lost their ability to bite, they slithered down the steps and disappeared into the bushes. Stuart's words had opened my eyes. I had a professional counselor now and I had Rob. I had found the antivenin.

34

THE YEAR

It's amazing what happens when your mind finally absorbs the cold hard fact that someone you loved could never be pleased. That no matter how hard you try, or work, or talk, the person will never be happy with you. The individual's happiness or lack of happiness is somehow independent of what you do, no matter how much effort you expend.

I woke the morning after my talk with Stuart much later than I expected. The clock said 10:18 a.m. It was a clear Saturday. Bright sunshine reflected off the ocean, and gulls flew overhead, keeping an eye out for edible trash. I lay quietly for a while and thought about the almost visible snakes that had slithered into the bushes...the lies and pain they'd inflicted on me for years. I thought about the ways I'd tried to facilitate Dayne's happiness and how I was never able to pull her across the line to contentment.

For the first time since Dayne left, I walked into my study, put my head in my hands, and cried. The house was quiet, and the sound of my sobs bounced against the walls. When my sobs diminished into sighs, I sat quietly and let my mind wander for a few minutes. Many evenings I had held MarLea as she cried in this very room, her depression as heavy as a blanket, smothering both of us. Those nights of tears were another opportunity for self-accusation—I couldn't make anyone happy. My daughter faced internal pain just like her mother, but today I realized the difference. Instead of berating me, MarLea had come to me and accepted my arms as her refuge. The walls of this study

157

had absorbed MarLea's pain and my sadness, but they had also reflected the sounds of beautiful music and well-written literature. Together MarLea and I had shared the sounds of music and tears, and sitting in the study together we felt safe. I knew these walls had good ears and wisdom enough to withhold judgment as they watched me crumble and cry alone.

MarLea and Matt appeared about an hour later. Nothing on my face or in my eyes betrayed my morning of crying, so there was no need to explain. I could still be the rock for my kids, and that was important to me. Matt was hungry and sweating after a morning bike ride. MarLea had spent the morning sleeping in.

"Hey, Dad," Matt said. "Can we get a pizza for lunch? I'm starving for pizza."

"Sure."

"OK, I'll call."

I watched my two kids head upstairs and realized things were almost normal again. In fact, they might be more normal now than any time in the past ten years. Matt was consumed with sports and studies, and MarLea was starting to see through the bouts of depression and glimpsing things that excited and inspired her. Within the past few months, she'd shown an interest in photography, so I'd bought her a camera for her birthday. Matt had an interest in doing a year abroad, so he and I had pored over websites outlining the options for international studies. To my great surprise, Matt was showing interest in international law.

Both kids communicated with their mother regularly, but consistently did so when I wasn't around. It worked well. For all the accusations Dayne had voiced while we were married, once the divorce was in process, she seemed to feel I was a good enough father to have primary custody of MarLea. Matt had turned eighteen, so as long as I paid his bills and he communicated with her periodically, Dayne was fine. I tried not to think about how simple it seemed for her to be happy now. But then again, if you had looked from the outside during all the years of our marriage, you would have thought she was content and happy then too. It made me wonder how Ted was faring inside the walls of their home, but truthfully I didn't care. It wasn't my place to care anymore. Dayne was his now. He could live with her happiness or her lack of it. That was between them.

The kids and I ate pizza then watched a movie. It was a comfortable afternoon, and I realized little by little, we were healing. Big wounds don't heal overnight. Given time, our emotional wounds were healing like any other wound. Healthy cells migrating toward each other and binding together. For me, healthy thoughts were binding with other healthy thoughts until there was a new layer of thinking to protect me from the pain of the raw memories. I was growing new skin.

I started to see myself from a different perspective. It definitely helped that I had a counselor who was assisting me in sorting out the truth. It also helped that I was interacting well with both my kids. Home was a safe place for us, and we were all healing, little by little. Of course, I still saw my flaws and they were many, but I no longer questioned if I was lazy, selfish, or stupid. Those words had lost their power over me—the power to make me question the core of my identity. I began to understand that counseling was giving me an opportunity to see the real Mike Passick and face up to the parts that needed change and the parts that could be accepted and appreciated.

Stuart had also helped me face one of my most annoying habits—comparing myself, ad nauseum, with Dayne's Ted and Brooke's Steve. These two men apparently had something I lacked, the ability to keep their women happy. I'd come to the illogical conclusion that I was missing some basic male attribute that accomplished this—some misshapen nucleotide in my DNA failed to satisfy women. My two high school romances that ended in nasty breakups gave birth to this belief, and it lived hidden inside me like a metastasis. It was time to identify the healthy cells and excise the malignant lies. I was exposing myself in counseling because I realized this therapy was for my benefit. I wasn't doing it to save a failing marriage. I was doing it to save me.

For the first time in over a year, I felt a palpable sense of hope. Maybe I could feel good again. Maybe I could finally decipher truth from error and discover better ways to interact in the future. Maybe, just maybe, I could find a place inside me that had room for love. If only I could kick the lingering sadness.

35

SEPTEMBER

About the time MarLea began her junior year, the relationship between Carol and Rob and me began to feel nearly normal again. Carol and Brooke had repaid the debt right on schedule, which allowed us to keep the focus on work and leave emotion out of the office. Brooke's checks had arrived regularly and when they stopped coming I missed seeing her signature at the bottom of each one. I wondered if she and Steve were happy. I wondered if I would hear they were honeymooning in Switzerland or Bali. Somehow it gave me a tiny bit of encouragement to know Brooke had found love even though my heart felt withered and empty.

As I traversed the steep climb of my divorce proceedings, Carol and Rob both offered their support. Carol somehow knew exactly when to make homemade muffins or bring something extra in her lunch so I wouldn't forget to eat. Rob hung around the office a bit longer some days and we'd talk for a while. He and Leanne invited me to dinner a couple of times a month when they knew I'd be home alone eating takeout. These and other little acts of kindness meant a lot to me.

Carol was the one who brought up Brooke late one afternoon in fall. Matt had just left for his second year of college. MarLea was immersed in high school and the independence of driving, gradually leaving her era of depression in puddles behind the car. Driving was something she enjoyed, and it gave her incentive to broaden her opportunities. I was adjusting to

161

the realization that my children were no longer dependent on me and in less than two years I'd be living in four thousand square feet by myself. I toyed with the idea of turning the kid's playroom into a billiards room, but rejected it for a much more realistic thought. Within two years, I'd probably sell the house, put that large family portrait and furniture the kids might need someday into storage, and move to a condo.

"Did I tell you Brooke is coming to visit me in two weeks?" Carol asked as she straightened her desk at the end of one workday.

"No," I said. "That'll be nice." My pulse quickened and I felt a familiar tingling in the Netherlands. Good thing I was sitting at my desk. Maybe I still had it.

"Yes," Carol said. "I didn't see much of her when she and Steve were together, but now that they've gone their separate ways, she's coming out for a visit."

I looked at Carol. She was turning off her computer and reaching for her purse. Clearly she didn't think this was important news, just casual conversation. Maybe she thought Brooke and I still talked. We didn't. I stood there waiting for Carol to continue, but she picked up the last of her things and walked toward the door.

"See you tomorrow," she said. "Have a good evening."

I went back into my office and sat down. That was interesting. Steve and Brooke weren't a couple anymore. Dayne and I weren't a couple anymore either. Officially, Brooke was available again. But did she want to hear from me? Had she sworn off men the way I'd been tempted to swear off women? Who could be sure love would ever work for me anyway? I had no confidence in my ability to be a successful husband, and I definitely had no confidence in my ability to be anyone's boyfriend. The word itself sounded like a bad fit for me, and the thought of dating made me cringe. It was so much easier to let my kids do the dating and focus on work. Three daters in one family would be one too many.

Brooke crossed my mind occasionally for the next two weeks, but I pushed those thoughts down a few times until they stopped bobbing to the surface. Easier to drown them than to allow them to stay afloat. Thoughts of Brooke were too distracting at work.

I was finishing a conference call when I heard Brooke's voice. She and Carol were talking just outside my office.

"I don't want to disturb him."

162

"Just wait till he's off the phone," Carol said.

I found a convenient way to finish the call. A few seconds later there was a knock.

"Got a minute?"

"Sure, come on in," I said. I walked around from behind my desk and reached out to shake Brooke's hand.

"Seriously?" she said with a laugh. Then she walked over and hugged me. "It's good to see you, Mike."

"Good to see you too, Brooke. How are things going?"

"Not bad. A little rough the last two months, but I'm getting my bearings again. How about you?"

"Things are good...yeah, they're good."

Brooke looked directly at me and rolled her eyes.

"It's been that long, huh?" she said. "Long enough for you to think I'd believe that?" She smiled that beautiful smile, the one that reflected concern without judgment.

"Apparently, I don't hide my emotions as well as I thought," I said.

"Oh, you hide them as well as any man," Brooke said. "But I have a spy in your office who knows better."

"Of course."

I nodded. Carol hadn't said much recently about Dayne leaving, but now that I thought about it, she had been bringing homemade muffins frequently. And I'd been eating them frequently, enjoying the distinctive taste of food made by a friend.

"So what has your spy told you?"

Brooke glanced around the room, walked over, and settled into a chair. She crossed her legs smoothly and laid both hands in her lap. I walked back to my desk and sat in my chair. Sunlight floated through the window, bouncing off the green flecks in Brooke's skirt. I noticed how nicely her skirt lay around her legs and under her hands.

"My spy," she said, "says you're doing a little better every day, but you still seem sad and lonely."

"Your spy is a good informant. That about describes it. Some days are sadder than others. Most days are just busy."

"I feel the same," Brooke said. "Busy seems to be the best antidote for sad."

"Yeah, until I attempt to sleep."

Brooke nodded.

"So," she said suddenly, "I didn't come here to talk about our mutual misery. I came to say hi...to let you know I was in town."

I smiled. One thing I appreciated about Brooke was the fact she could be frank and gentle at the same time.

"Did you happen to come by to see if I'd invite you to lunch tomorrow?" I asked.

"Maybe"

I waited. She smiled.

"Where would you like me to meet you?" she asked playfully.

"Old Town Deli?"

"Perfect," she said. "I'll see you there tomorrow at noon."

The place was packed when we walked in the next day. Harried wait staff weaved between the tables balancing large trays of potpies, deli sandwiches, and coleslaw. The scent of dill pickles and garlic dawdled behind every tray, permeating the entire restaurant. Patrons were packed into booths and overflowed onto extra chairs. We stood just inside the doorway beside an older couple who smelled like baby powder and lavender, and a group of women with large purses who were trading stories about their kids. It wasn't quite the environment I would have chosen for a business lunch, but it effectively kept Brooke pushed up against me. She felt comfortable and smelled nice. If her smell included perfume, it was subtle.

Ten minutes later we settled into opposite sides of a booth. Loud groups on either side made conversation challenging but private. No one was going to hear us over their noise.

"We haven't talked in a long time, Mike. I'd really like to know how you're doing."

"I'd like to hear what's happened with you too. It feels like we've lived decades since we talked last."

"It does," she said. "OK, I'll start. Steve and I were really serious. I thought he was the one...a great guy, kind and considerate with a good job. He said all the right things at the beginning. We had a wonderful, almost perfect romance. We traveled, connected in all the right ways, and talked about marriage. But one night over dinner, without prelude, he told me it was over."

My eyes widened.

"Yeah. My reaction exactly," she said. "He said he felt hemmed in by the thought of spending the rest of his life with one woman, and he'd decided it was time to date around again. Fortunately, I had the courage and chutzpah to simply say, 'Have a great life. I wish you the best,' then stand up and walk out."

"Classy move," I said.

"It's amazing what I can do when pushed into a corner," Brooke said. "He sent my things over in a cab later that evening. And…" She hesitated and looked up for a moment. "And that was it. A very abrupt, painful ending to what I thought was the perfect relationship. Frankly, I feel like an idiot."

"Why?" I asked.

"Are you serious?"

"Yeah…why do you feel like an idiot?"

"Because I walked right into another relationship with a man who didn't want me! You'd think I'd be smarter than that, but no…I just keep making the same mistake."

Her voice was harsh. The muscles in her jaw were tight as ropes. Her eyes had just enough moisture to glisten, but not enough to produce a full-fledged tear. She looked angry and fatigued. I recognized those feelings and reached across the table to touch her hand. Without looking directly at me, she let her hand rest under mine for a few seconds and then patted my hand briefly and withdrew to her own side of the table.

"So," she said quickly, looking directly at me now. "That's my story. How about yours?"

"Mine is just as depressing," I said, trying to be playful, but realizing the truth of my statement. "I knew my marriage was dead, but I thought maybe we could find a way to resuscitate the corpse. Instead of focusing on our family, like I was trying to do, Dayne was busy finding another guy to meet her needs, presumably in ways I couldn't. If you feel like an idiot, I feel like a guy with a huge 'Loser' written all over my forehead. My former wife is living it up with another guy who lives five miles away. She told me our marriage was over and didn't even spend one night in a hotel. She just moved in with good ole Teddy-boy."

Brooke looked at me with sad eyes. The muscles in my neck and face felt tense and hot.

"Wow," I said. "I didn't even realize I had that much anger left after this long."

"We're both pretty pathetic, aren't we?" Brooke smiled weakly. The food came just in time to save us. We ate slowly, attempting a conversation about my kids even though it was obvious we were both lost in our own thoughts. Halfway through the meal, Brooke reached across the table and took my hand.

"You know, Mike," she said, "I had some unrealistic hope that having lunch with you would help me get over Steve faster. I thought perhaps your feelings weren't still raw from your divorce. But clearly, that isn't the case. We're both deeply wounded, and until we take the time to heal individually, we don't stand any chance of being in a healthy relationship with each other or anyone else."

"We were just venting. I'm sure we could find better things to talk about."

"Maybe," she said. "But the truth is, neither of us has healed yet. You're carrying your heart around in pieces, and I've got mine under lock and key. There's room for friendship here, Mike, but I'm really not interested in friends with benefits."

"Did I ever suggest that?" I asked, slightly hurt.

"No. But I'm not a fool. We have chemistry, and it'll ignite again as soon as we spend any time together. Look," she said firmly, "let's just say we had a nice lunch and go our separate ways. You and I have a good friendship. Let's not mess it up."

She flagged down our server and dropped her credit card on the bill as soon as it came. I didn't even have time to reach for my wallet.

"I'm happy to pay," I said.

"If you don't mind, I'd rather," she said. "It'll make this feel less like a date and more like a business lunch."

"So in a matter of minutes, we've gone from friends to business associates?"

"I don't want to complicate our lives, Mike. You've got a lot of healing to do. So do I. Let's focus on what's most important."

They were the most abrupt words I'd ever heard from Brooke. For a moment she seemed like a stern teacher admonishing a reluctant student.

166

As soon as the server returned, she signed the restaurant copy, put the receipt in her purse, and stood up.

"Come on," she said, with the slightest insinuation of kindness. "I'll walk with you to our cars."

We walked past the families celebrating birthdays, the coworkers laughing together, and the moms and kids buying cinnamon rugelach. I felt a sadness wrap itself around me like an overcoat. I couldn't remember another time I'd felt so completely, utterly alone. Even the older couple who smelled like baby powder and lavender had each other. I didn't even have Brooke as a fallback friend anymore. She was about to drive away, and I had no idea if I'd even see her again.

"It was nice to see you, Brooke," I said as we walked side by side, yet miles apart. "I do enjoy being your friend and I hope we'll stay in touch."

"I enjoy it too," she said softly. "I'm just afraid of anything that involves us right now. We both need some space to heal."

We walked to her car and I just stood there, not knowing whether to hug her good-bye or offer my hand. She dug in her purse for keys then gave me a quick, impersonal hug before she slipped into the driver's seat. I watched as she pulled out of the parking lot into the flow of traffic. I thought I saw her brush the back of her hand across her cheek, but I couldn't be sure. She wasn't facing me.

I drove back to the office via the beach route, mostly because I didn't want to see Carol or Rob quite yet. The sun was blindingly bright, reflecting off the water and the windshields of other cars. What should have been an enjoyable drive became difficult and frustrating as I tried to see brake lights and traffic signals. I barely missed hitting a guy in a blue SUV who slammed on his brakes in front of me. I didn't expect such a hard stop.

36
OCTOBER

For days I felt as if the wind had been knocked out of me. Somewhere inside me, I'd always held the belief that Brooke would be a constant in my life. Maybe not my wife or my lover, but the one woman I could count on to stick around. I was fine with phone calls, but I wasn't sure if she'd felt the same way anymore, so I didn't call. Truth was, I felt a little anger over the way she'd turned a venting session, a "tell me how you're doing" invitation, into a reason to bolt. It felt a little too reminiscent of Dayne's tactics. But as I thought about the comparison, I couldn't help but notice Brooke never once insulted or berated me. She didn't call me names or tell me I was weak for expressing my feelings. She wasn't cruel to me, but she kicked me in the balls anyway. It hurt and I decided it was time to face reality. Hang up the spurs, cowboy. The rodeo is over. You won't be riding again.

Work was the most constant lover I'd ever known, so I returned to her arms. Work whispered to me that I was successful. She complimented me every day, and rewarded me with money. She was always ready to receive me and never turned me away. At the end of the day, when all the other women in my life had betrayed or abandoned me, work stood patiently waiting for me to return to her without condemnation. Yet somehow she was an empty shell of a woman.

I never talked with Stuart or Rob about work as my security or about Brooke's quick departure. I wish I had sometimes, but it just never came up. With other guys, it was easy to avoid a difficult subject.

During those weeks and months after Brooke's visit, I tried not to think much. I just worked. MarLea and I had a good routine at home. She'd fix dinner if she was home in the afternoon and I'd clean up the dishes. MarLea had lots of friends, and she'd call me every afternoon to let me know where she was headed after her last class. Now that she was driving, it was easy to let her determine her own schedule and just inform me. Matt was thriving in college, so it was easy to focus on work. The kids seemed fine. Or so I thought until I got the phone call from Brandon's mother one afternoon.

"Mr. Passick?"

"Yes."

"You're MarLea's father, right?"

"Yes."

"This is Brandon Richards's mom. Bonnie. Our kids are in the same class."

There was a pause.

"I need to let you know I found your daughter and my son upstairs this afternoon...in his bedroom..."

My heart instantly sank. I was sure I knew what was coming next, and my mind was already walking down the aisle of the pharmacy looking for pregnancy kits. Honestly, she was barely buying tampons four years ago, and now this...

"...they were on the bed..."

Get it out! What were they doing?

"...with pills spread out...I think they were experimenting with drugs."

It took me a minute to realize she wasn't talking pregnancy—she was talking medication.

"Uh, Mrs. Richards," I said, "do you know where they got the pills?"

"Yes...my father had surgery last spring. He had some oxycodone in the downstairs medicine cabinet."

"Is there any chance they overdosed?" I asked, suddenly aware of that risk.

"I don't think so," she said. "He only had about ten left. It was your daughter, my son, and a couple of other kids. I'm calling their parents too. I just don't believe this. The kids said they only took two each, and according to the poison center, that's not too much unless they do take more right away." Her voice trailed off and there was silence on the other end of the phone.

"Mr. Passick," she said, "should I call an ambulance? I know you're a lawyer. Am I going to be sued if I don't call nine one one?"

"I don't know, Mrs. Richards. I'm not a doctor, and the best I know is poison control's recommendation. I'm not going to sue you, if that's what you're asking."

There was more silence.

"Do you know where my daughter is right now? Has she left your house?"

"No, she's right here. We told the kids they couldn't leave until I talked with each set of parents. They can't be driving with drugs in their system."

"Good," I said. "Would you please take her keys? I'll come get her."

"Of course."

I hung up the phone, grabbed my coat, turned the lights off in my office, and drove to the Richardses' house. There were two cars out front already.

A tall blond woman in a pair of jeans and a sweater opened the door seconds after I knocked. Behind her, a father was escorting his son to the door. I didn't recognize either one. Neither looked happy.

"I'm Bonnie," the woman said, extending her hand to shake mine. "Brandon's mom."

"I'm Mike Passick," I said. "MarLea's dad."

"I know. We met a few years ago at a school open house. Your wife and I were in yoga together."

I nodded. "My former wife," I said.

"Oh," Bonnie said. She turned around and walked toward the kitchen, motioning me to follow. MarLea was sitting on a bar stool, watching as I walked in.

"I'm sorry, Dad," she said, moving the bar stool aside to hug me.

I didn't know what a good parent was supposed to do. I wasn't sure if I should be angry, if I should start taking away privileges so Bonnie could see I was doing the right thing. I just wasn't sure what to do, so I hugged her back.

"Let's go home, MarLea," I said. "We'll discuss this later."

"What about my car, Dad?"

"I'm sure it'll be fine on the street until we figure things out." I looked at Bonnie and she nodded.

"OK," MarLea said.

I took MarLea's keys from Bonnie and put them in my pocket. MarLea and Bonnie began walking toward the front door, gathering personal items and putting them into MarLea's backpack. As I walked through the living room toward the front door, I heard a deep male voice behind me. I hadn't seen anyone sitting there.

"So what ya gonna do with that young'un?"

I turned to see an older gentleman sitting in a dark leather recliner with an open book on his lap. The afternoon light was beginning to fade, and the last streaks of sunlight filtered through the pale curtains. He reached up and adjusted the reading lamp behind his chair.

"I'm not sure," I said.

"Thinkin' a groundin' 'er?"

"Maybe."

"Don't do it."

Bonnie and MarLea were already at the front door waiting for me.

"Bonnie, darlin', y'all go on into the kitchen a minute an' lemme have a word with Mike, aw' right?"

"Sure, Dad," Bonnie said. "Don't be long though."

The older man stood up and extended his hand.

"Name's Jim," he said. "I'm Bonnie's dad."

I stood there a moment looking at this interesting man. He was the exact opposite of his daughter, who was blond and long legged. Jim couldn't have been more than five six. He was as round as she was thin, as dark haired as she was blond.

"Looks like her mother," he said with a laugh. "But believe me, that little gal got half my genes. You'll see 'em if she ever gets mad. I just got lucky to fall in love with a Swedish beauty and have a daughter who don't look a thing like me!" He laughed heartily at his own humor. I smiled.

172

"So back to the question at hand," Jim said. "Whadda you plan to do with that little gal a' yours? 'Specially since you got ta figure it out on your own?"

I looked at him sideways.

"Seen it a million times, son. You single fathers have a distinct look about ya. Look just blazes out, 'M' wife took off and left me with this teenage girl. What the hell am I 'spose ta do with 'er?'"

I smiled. "It's that obvious?"

"Oh yeah, son. You single dads are easier ta pick out than a pros'tute on Fifteenth Street. Mind if I give ya a bit of advice, seein' as how I sat on the bench of juvenil' court in Waco, Texas, for over thirty years and know a thing or two 'bout teenagers?"

"You're a judge?"

"Was one. Over thirty years. Didn't have ta be a lawyer in those days ta sit on a bench. Ya just had to have a lil' common sense, be willin' ta read the law and know howda hold a gavel. D'cided I'd rather do that than sit on a tractor all day, so I hired some hands on m' ranch and began judgin'. Was a good life."

I smiled again. Just my luck to walk into a house with a judge on site. Actually, maybe it was better luck than I thought.

"So what's your advice? I'm all ears."

"Well," he said, "last thing ya wanna do is ground 'er. She's sixteen, for goo'ness' sake, and them sixteen-yur-olds c'n find trouble on ev'ry shelf a' their closet. If ya ground her, she's jus' gonna get bored. In my 'pinion, boredom spells d'saster fur the young. I say…keep 'em busy."

"Grounding a kid never made a lot of sense to me, but it's what most parents seem to do these days."

"Workin' well for 'em, isn't it!" he said powerfully. "It's a damn stupid idea."

"So what do you suggest?"

"Ya know, when I's on the bench, I used to make them kids work. If a kid stole somethin' at the store, I'd make him repay it by cleanin' a sidewalk or sweepin' a floor. Kid wrote somethin' in spray paint on the side of a buildin', I'd make 'em clean it off 'n paint the high school or a nursin' home."

"Did it work?"

173

"Sometimes. Much as any punishment c'n work when they's other factors involved. Once had a kid ask ta' paint a mural on the dinin' room wall down at the old folk's home. Was nice when he finished. I wodden'a guessed he was an artist, but he was."

"So you think I should make MarLea work off taking medication?"

"Think you should come up with somethin' memorable, not borin'. Somethin' ta make her think 'bout what she done."

"Thank you, Jim," I said. I walked over and shook his hand as he stood next to his chair. "You have a lot of wisdom. I only wish all judges were as levelheaded as you."

"Why, thank ya," he said. "I hear yur daughter say yur a lawyer?"

"Yes, sir."

"Why don't ya drop by now and then and catch me up on all the legal cases I hear 'bout on TV?"

"I'd enjoy that," I said. "Let me deal with my daughter, and then maybe we can talk again."

I walked back into the kitchen to retrieve MarLea.

"I hope my dad wasn't too intrusive," Bonnie said.

"Not at all," I said. "He's an interesting guy."

"That he is!" Bonnie said. "Try raising a sixteen-year-old boy under his nose. It's an experience. I'll probably sit down with him tonight and decide how to deal with Brandon after this mess."

"We'll all spend tonight dealing with this mess," I said as MarLea followed me to the door. "I appreciate your wise handling of the immediate situation, Bonnie. Thank you."

MarLea sat silently in the passenger seat as we drove home, then she gathered her things and walked into the house. She sat on the barstool and looked at me.

"I'm really sorry, Dad," she said. "I don't know what we were thinking."

"I've wondered the same thing," I said. "What in the world were you thinking? Someone could have died. Can you imagine how you'd feel?"

"I know, Dad. I'm so sorry."

I sat silently next to her for a few minutes, then I got up and paced.

"Look, MarLea. I'm no parenting expert. I need to call your mom and let her know what happened. Maybe she'll have some ideas on how to deal with this. In the meantime, I'm taking your keys, because right now you're not making good choices about where you go and what you do. And I'm pretty sure you'll be volunteering your time somewhere next Saturday and Sunday."

"Dad, I said I was sorry."

"I'm glad you're sorry," I said. "I'm also glad you're not dead."

MarLea went to her room. She didn't seem terribly angry, which was a small relief. I called Dayne and left a voice mail. She called back the next morning after I'd dropped MarLea off at school.

"Why are you calling me, Mike?" she said abruptly.

"I'm calling to let you know MarLea was involved in some unprescribed medication use last night. She and a few friends took some oxycodone."

"What?" Dayne nearly screamed into the phone. "What in the world were you doing while she was doing drugs with her friends?"

"I was working, Dayne," I said sharply. "I work in the afternoon."

"Of course," she said. "You always work. Why should I be surprised? Have you taken her to a doctor?"

"No."

"Why not?" Dayne's voice was full of fury. "What kind of stupid father finds his kid overdosing and doesn't take her to a doctor?"

"Dayne, stop. First, poison control said there was no immediate risk of overdose with this amount of oxycodone. She'll be all right. Second, I'm not going to continue this conversation if you keep shouting." I decided to try a tactic Stuart had taught me. Don't fight back. Don't get angry. Set a boundary.

Dayne lowered her voice, but the rage was thick.

"Mike" she said, "you are fully responsible for MarLea's safety and well-being when she's under your care. As an attorney you obviously know exactly what I mean when I say that. If anything—and I mean *anything*—ever happens to my daughter on your watch, I will hire the best attorney on the planet and destroy you. Just because I'm not with her every day doesn't mean I'm not watching."

"Look, Dayne, I called to keep you informed, not to argue with you," I said, realizing there was nothing I could say in response, nothing I could do to assure Dayne I was doing my very best to be a good dad. How could I possibly reassure her I was a good father when in her mind I had been a terrible husband? It was fruitless. "I called to let you know what happened

175

and to let you know I'm taking MarLea's car away for two weeks and arranging for her to do community service this weekend."

"Fine," Dayne said. "Ted and I are leaving for Seattle tomorrow morning. Just make sure she's not experimenting with more drugs. You are the parent in charge, Mike. Act like it."

"I'll do that," I said. "Good-bye."

I wanted to add "thanks for your support" or "kiss my ass" or "hope the plane to Seattle breaks open like a tin can and sucks you right out of your seat," but I didn't. At least not out loud.

37

OCTOBER

MarLea had a study group at Brandon's house a week later. I walked her to the door and asked Bonnie what time I needed to pick MarLea up. The minute Jim heard my voice, he came up behind Bonnie.

"Hey there, Mike, do ya have to rush off ta somethin'mportant?"

"Just the usual stuff."

"Well, why don't you join me in the living room for a spell? Heard a piece on CNN 'bout prison overcrowdin' that just boils my shorts, and I'd love ta talk about it wi' someone 'sides Bonnie. She tires of listenin' to my observations and 'pinions."

"Not true, Dad," Bonnie said. "But Mike may have other plans."

"Tell you what, Jim," I said. "I have to run to Target to pick up some paper towels and deodorant, but if you want to come along, I'd be happy for the company."

"Lemme get m' coat," he said.

The minute we were in the car, Jim began talking about prison overcrowding, a case before the Supreme Court regarding the legality of narcotics checkpoints, and an article he'd read about nonindigenous carp invading Lake Erie. I was fascinated by his expertise and country wisdom, but I also enjoyed the personal stories he threw in every now and then. At the end of one story, he looked over my way and asked, "Did ya have a good dad,

Mike? I'm not tryin' ta pry, but I'm just askin' 'cause ya look ta me like you're tryin' ta be a good dad and you're havin' ta blaze a new trail."

"Now, what makes you say that?"

"Am I wrong?"

"No, but what makes you say that?"

"Don' know," he said. "Lot a' years on the bench. Seein' a lot of men tryin' to improve on their fathers' rotten examples. Ya just remind me a' some a' them. Tha's all."

"You have amazing insight," I said. "My father was an abusive man, and I'm doing everything I can to avoid his pattern."

Jim didn't say anything more. He just rode in silence for a while, looking out at the heavily populated Southern California landscape.

"Beats me," he said suddenly, "why ya crazy Californians are willin' ta pay so much for a little bitty piece a land just 'cause it looks out on the ocean. You're so damn close, you could pass soap from one house to the other in the mornin', and yet ya pay millions a dollars for raw land. Not even a house, just land. It's crazy."

I smiled. He was right. It was crazy, but it was reality. That ocean view was worth many, many millions of dollars. I knew because I owned a piece of it. And Jim was right. I could almost reach across from my shower window to my neighbor's and pass the soap in the morning. Funny thing. It made so much sense when Dayne and I bought the house. Now sitting alone in that big house with the million-dollar view had less appeal to me. It wasn't nearly as enjoyable as talking with an old Texas judge on the way to Target.

I parked and waited as Jim got out of the car. It was obvious he had hip trouble, because he rose slowly and walked at a much slower pace than my usual rush. He rubbed a spot on his thigh periodically, so I purposely slowed down to let him find a comfortable, slower stride.

"Ever bought one a' them rice cookers?" Jim asked as we headed back to find paper towels.

"Yeah. I have one."

"Now, help me understand why you'd want to buy somethin' that's just the same as a pot. You just put rice and water in, right? Jus' like a pot?"

"Yes, you just put in rice and water, but it doesn't burn, and it'll keep the rice warm for quite a few hours. That's handy sometimes."

Jim nodded as he looked at the aisle of rice cookers and slow cookers.

"I can see the advantage," he said. "I can see that."

We walked by an aisle of brightly colored melamine plates—orange, lime green, and bright pink.

"I'd think," he said, "those plates would make reg'lar food look anemic. How's a simple potato s'pposed to compete with that?"

I just smiled. We found the paper towels, and I grabbed a package from the middle shelf. I noticed Jim was interested in the people around him. He was obviously a keen observer of humanity, and I was interested to see if he'd say anything more. A few seconds later, he leaned toward me. With the lift of his chin and a motion of his eyes, he pointed to a man and a little girl. The man was about my age, maybe a few years younger. He was dressed in jeans and a polo shirt. Beside him, a girl about six years old was dressed in a pink tutu and an orange T-shirt. She wore sneakers with no socks, and she was adorable. Holding her dad's hand, she leaned over the paper plates and paper cups, carefully inspecting each package.

"Weekend dad on the biweekly visit," Jim said. "He's a good one. That lil' gal will be aw right."

I realized I'd probably walked by a hundred dads just like myself without ever realizing it. We might be in the same situation, single dads, but somehow we didn't feel the connection. Frankly, I was just trying to survive and help my kids make it to adulthood without some permanent injury. It struck me that this guy was probably trying to do the same thing.

Jim had moved on as I stood thinking. He was at the end of the aisle headed toward the pharmacy section, where I could pick up my deodorant. When I caught up to him, he pointed across the aisle toward two older teens looking at cards.

"They'll be aw right too," he said. "Doesn't matter they got jeans hangin' down their butts. Doesn't even matter they prob'ly should be studyin' right now. They're over pickin' out a birthday card for Mom, and they're not just grabbin' the first one either. They're takin' their time to find just the right one. They'll be aw right in the long haul."

Jim's wisdom fascinated me. He saw detail I never took the time to notice, and he had an interest in people I tended to ignore.

"I'll bet you were a good judge," I said, wondering if he'd push off the compliment.

179

"I was," he said. "Good, jus' not always right."

I gathered my deodorant and we headed to the checkout area. It was almost eight o'clock, and the store was thinning out. A few registers were open, manned by tired employees who couldn't wait to end their shift.

"Howdy," Jim said to the exhausted woman behind the counter.

"Hi," she said. "Did you find everything OK?"

"Think so," he replied.

She scanned our two items and waited while I dug out my credit card.

"Got any kids?" Jim asked.

"Yeah." She looked at him and smiled. "Two."

"Be sure and hug 'em tonight."

"I always do. Every night when I get home," she said.

"Good," Jim said, looking directly into her face. "Tha's good."

I took the receipt and turned to leave.

"Have a nice night," she said, looking at Jim.

"Thank ya, ma'am," Jim said with a little nod of his head. "Love up those kids now."

"I will."

We drove back to Bonnie's house talking about cattle and California's approach to business law. As we parked and began walking toward the door, I realized I rarely greeted MarLea with a hug when I came home. For whatever reason, I just usually walked in the house, dropped my briefcase in my office, and headed to the kitchen. MarLea would be cooking or upstairs in her room. I was often watching TV or in my study when she went to bed. Sometime she'd give me a kiss on the cheek before she headed upstairs, but more often, she'd just wander up with a "Good night, Dad" from the top of the stairs.

When was the last time I purposely hugged MarLea? I wondered. Then I remembered. It was when she hugged me at Bonnie's house, hoping I wasn't mad. She had initiated the hug, not me.

I walked into Bonnie's house behind Jim.

"Hi, hun'," Jim said loudly. "We're back."

"Hi, Dad, we're all in the kitchen."

Jim and I walked through the living room into the kitchen, where Bonnie was setting out another bowl of popcorn and the kids were studying around the table.

180

"No-studying-in-the-bedroom policy now," Bonnie whispered to me. I nodded.

"How's it going?" I asked MarLea as I walked over and put my hand on her shoulder. She reached up and covered my hand with hers.

"Good," she said. "We'll be done in about ten minutes."

"Would you and Dad like some popcorn?" Bonnie asked.

"I'm good. Thanks though."

"Me too," Jim said.

He and I walked back into the living room and sat down.

"Thanks fur the Target run," Jim said. "Nice ta get out now an' then, since I ain't 'spose ta drive yet."

I shot a questioning look his direction.

"Had a li'l issue with m' right hip, and doc says I need ta let it settle a bit 'fore I drive. Somethin' about slow reaction time."

"Probably a good idea," I said.

"Aw, maybe." Jim sounded unconvinced. "I gotta do it, or Bonnie'll take away m' keys too."

He laughed at his own joke and then settled into his chair with some effort. About the time he got settled, MarLea appeared with her backpack slung across one shoulder.

"All set, Dad."

"Good night, Jim," I said.

"'Night. Drop by again sometime."

"I will."

That night I made a point to hug MarLea before she headed upstairs.

"I love you, Dad," she said as she turned toward the stairs. "You're a good dad. Thanks for taking me tonight."

"I love you too, MarLea," I said. "Thanks for being a great daughter. I'm glad I went."

38

NOVEMBER

I drove MarLea to Bonnie's house twice during her "no driving weeks." I found it enjoyable to hang out with Jim, and surprisingly I found Bonnie's kitchen comforting and warm as the nights grew colder. There were usually smells in that kitchen, some sweet, some pungent, many lingering from dinner. Many of those smells reminded me of my mother's cooking.

The week MarLea got her keys back, she headed over to Brandon's house again to study chemistry on Thursday night. I expected her back around nine. I was watching TV when the phone rang.

"Hi, Dad."

"Hi, sis."

"I'm over at Brandon's house; you know that right?"

"Right."

"Well, do you know how to fix a leak under the kitchen sink? Because Mrs. Richards doesn't know, and her dad can't crawl under there, and none of us kids know. I told her you might."

"Doesn't her husband know how to fix it?" I asked.

"None on site," MarLea said in code. "Doesn't exist."

"Oh."

I had assumed there was a Mr. Richards. I was sure I'd seen a wedding ring on Bonnie's finger.

"So, Dad, can you fix it? Can you come over and look, please? Water is coming out."

"Sure. I'll be right there."

I grabbed my jacket and headed over to Bonnie's house. She was waiting by the door, and we walked quickly into the house.

"Thanks so much for coming, Mike. This is just what I need before the holidays."

First check the supply lines, and then check the drain lines, I reminded myself. The dishwasher was running, and under the sink a trickle of water dripped off the garbage disposal. There was a good-sized puddle inside the cabinet.

"Got any old towels?"

"Sure. Let me turn this off so we can hear." Bonnie opened the dishwasher door and headed toward another room.

I took the towels Bonnie handed me to wipe up the standing water then grabbed a dry towel to wipe the water off the disposal. No drip reappeared.

"That's strange," I said. I'd assumed the problem was the garbage disposal. One of my early-years-of-marriage houses had a disposal that leaked, and I had all kinds of problems finding the source.

I ran water down the sink—a lot of water down the sink—and still no leak. I was just about to give up and suggest she call a real plumber when I remembered the dishwasher had been running when I walked in. Bonnie had opened it to stop the noise.

"Could you turn on the dishwasher for me?" I asked. Bonnie looked puzzled but closed the dishwasher door.

I looked under the sink and listened to the dishwasher pump water out of the line. After a few seconds, the drip reappeared.

"OK," I said. "I think I know the culprit." I crawled deeper under the sink until I could run my hand up the hose from the garbage disposal to the air gap. There was a distinctive wet spot where the hose and the air gap met.

"Shut off the dishwasher again for me, please," I said from deep under the sink. I realized Bonnie, Jim, and the kids were all gathered around my legs waiting. I heard someone open the dishwasher door. I reached up and disconnected the two hoses—one from the dishwasher to the air gap and one from the air gap to the disposal. I emerged from under the sink, pulled the cover off the air gap at the top of the sink, and unscrewed the locking nut. The air gap fell to the floor of the cabinet. Everyone looked at me.

"Here's the problem," I said. "A crack in the outflow pipe of the air gap. I'll be back in a few with a new one."

Jim walked behind me as I headed out the door to my car.

"Where'd ya learn to do that, son?" he asked.

"My dad," I said quickly. "He was pretty handy around the house. Could fix most things."

"Hmmm," Jim said. "Guess he wasn't all bad."

"No," I said, turning to look at him. "I guess not."

Forty minutes later, Bonnie had a dripless sink, and I felt as if I'd done my good deed for the week.

"Thanks so much, Mike," Bonnie said as I washed my hands and gathered the tools she'd brought from her garage. "Since Dad's surgery, I don't have my regular handyman."

"Glad I could help," I said.

She reached for a container inside the fridge and handed it to me.

"Here," she said. "Something for your lunch tomorrow. Homemade chicken pot pie."

"You don't have to do that," I said.

"Please take it, Mike. I'm really grateful for your help. You saved me at least a hundred dollars, and to be truthful, my chicken pot pie sells for about that. So we're even."

"Thanks," I said, smiling.

Bonnie walked with me out to the garage, where we put tools back into her dad's workbench.

"Bonnie," I said, "if it's not too personal, do you mind me asking about your wedding ring? MarLea said there isn't a Mr. Richards."

"There was," she said. "I wear my mom's wedding ring on my finger and mine around my neck because my mother and my husband both died in the same car accident two years ago. He was taking her to the doctor, the traffic stopped suddenly, someone hit them at seventy and pushed them into the back of an eighteen-wheeler."

"I'm so sorry," I said. "I remember hearing someone in MarLea's class lost a dad and grandmother in a car wreck, but I didn't realize that was your family."

"It was," she said. "My dad and I decided it would be easier on all of us if we lived together for a while. We needed each other. It's been two years of grief and sadness."

"I'm sure it's been really hard."

"Harder than you can imagine," Bonnie said. "But fortunately, there are wonderful friends and neighbors like you who make life a little easier. I'm really grateful, not just for your plumbing expertise, but also for befriending my dad."

"I enjoy your dad," I said truthfully. "He's an interesting guy. And I'm glad I could fix the problem tonight. It really wasn't that complicated. You just had to know where to look."

"Glad you knew!"

I nodded slightly and smiled.

"The kids will be done soon," Bonnie said. "I'll make sure MarLea heads home around nine."

"Thanks," I said as I got into my car. "Good night, Bonnie."

"Good night, Mike. Thanks again."

I drove back home thinking about the differences between burying a husband and mother at the same time and watching a wife walk into the arms of another man. There were such sharp contrasts, but the look I saw in Bonnie's eyes, the look of sadness and grief, was the same look I'd seen in my own mirror. Jim had never said a thing about his wife's death, so I hadn't known until tonight that Bonnie, Jim, and I were all in stages of grief at the same time.

Sad eyes may occur for different reasons, but they still look the same. Broken hearts may come in all shapes and sizes and occur for myriad reasons, but those of us who grieve have more in common than we realize. If only we could figure out how to cross the canyon of grief-induced isolation, we might find a friend.

186

39

DECEMBER

Thanksgiving came and went that year with minimal fanfare. Matt spent Thanksgiving with his roommate's family in Maryland, and MarLea and I spent the afternoon with Rob and Leanne's family watching football and eating until we were stuffed. Ted and Dayne were in Cabo. The second Sunday in December, MarLea and I picked up a tree from the local nursery and spent the evening decorating the tree with the Trans-Siberian Orchestra and Josh Groban providing holiday music. I didn't want to be Scrooge too many years in a row.

I hadn't sent out or even thought about Christmas cards since Dayne left, so I was surprised to get one from Brooke. It came in a red envelope with her name and return address in handwritten script. At first I wondered what it could be; then I remembered it was December. The card was a photo of Brooke standing in a lush forest. She had a backpack casually slung over her shoulder, and her hair framed her face in gentle curls. She looked playful, as if she'd been bounding up the trail laughing just a moment before. The printed text at the bottom said "Merry Christmas from Costa Rica. Hope you have a wonderful holiday season with family and friends. Best wishes, Brooke." I instantly wondered who'd taken the picture. A new boyfriend? A fellow traveler? The picture gave no hints. I turned the card over and saw her handwriting.

187

"Hi, Mike. My friend Sarah and I decided to travel instead of dreading the holidays alone. I'll be back at Mom and Dad's for Christmas dinner. Call sometime if you want. I miss our talks. Brooke."

While the note was definitely an improvement over our last conversation, it still felt guarded. *Call if you want. No pressure. No real need. Just if you have some extra time and aren't inconvenienced. If you don't call, it won't be that big a deal. Because after all, I don't really need you, Mike. I have other friends. You're not that special.* Suddenly I realized how far my mind was taking five simple sentences. But I didn't fully understand why. Yes, I was hurt when Brooke suddenly turned my words into a reason to end our lunch together. But why did my mind take me to a place of self-recrimination, a place of diminished worth?

The holidays ended and our house routine resumed. Matt went back to college after being home for winter break. MarLea immersed herself in high school life again. I worked, played golf, and waited for the days to lengthen. Coming home hours after dark made the nights feel long and lonely, even with music.

MarLea studied with Brandon, Connor, and Kate every Thursday in an attempt to absorb chemistry before every Friday's quiz. Jim and I found reasons to talk periodically throughout that winter. He'd call about a home project, or I'd call for advice about parenting a seventeen-year-old daughter. In late April, he mentioned Bonnie wanted a patio cover and he thought he'd better get it done before the hot weather.

"We're not in Texas, Jim," I said. "It won't get hotter than eighty until August."

"Yup, I know, but the sun shines hard on this ole head, and I ain't found a hat that can keep me cool anymore, even in eighty degrees." Jim cleared his throat. I realized he might be asking for help in a gentlemanly way.

"Would you like some help?"

"Oh, I wouldn't wanna inconvenience ya."

"I think I'd enjoy building something, working with my hands."

"Well, only if you c'n spare the time."

"I can," I said. "Do you think we could finish it in a week? I might take two weeks off and head to Tahoe with the kids afterward."

Jim laughed. "There's a time I could've finished a lil' project like this in a coupla days, but no more. I think with both of us workin', we can get it done in five days so you c'n take that trip."

188

I pulled out my calendar. "How does the week of June sixteenth look for you? Matt will be home from college that Thursday, so the timing could work."

"Other than a doctor's appointment Friday mornin', I'm wide open."

"I'll put it on my calendar."

As Jim and I began planning the patio cover, I found more reasons to be at Bonnie's house. She was always friendly and kind, yet somehow sadness still gathered around her. She smiled often, but it was the smile of weighted muscles and sodden cheeks. I found myself wanting to reach for her hand, to comfort her, to pull her out of all that sadness and save her from drowning. But I wasn't strong enough myself yet. So I just smiled back and enjoyed her home-cooked meals when I was invited to stay. Her hugs of greeting and homemade meals keep me from starving.

Once Jim and I started working on the actual project—buying the materials, pouring the concrete footings—our conversations drifted from subject to subject. We talked about politics, children, technology, space exploration, and life in general. The only subject Jim avoided was sex.

"Can't see any reason why that dang TV's pouring out sex all the time," he said one afternoon as we discussed new shows we'd seen on TV. "There's a reason they's doors on bedrooms. It's a private thing 'tween two people, not somethin' for spewin' all over."

"Some people might call that an old-fashioned view of sexuality," I said.

Jim looked directly at me, shovel in his hand. He wiped his glove across his forehead, creating a broad streak of sweaty dirt.

"If it's old-fashioned ta love one woman, ta keep just 'tween us the one thing we shared no one else can bust in on or mess up, then I guess I'm old-fashioned. Hell, I've been called worse. But let me tell ya, son, there ain't nobody gonna get me ta talk about that sweet love I shared with my wife. Was too special. Would feel like desicratin' her mem'ry."

Case closed. I had no intention of stomping on the grave of a dead woman. That night I thought about that kind of love. Had I ever experienced it? Probably not. Did I think I would find it one day? Probably not. Reality was reality. My life hadn't been filled with that kind of love, and I had no prospects on the horizon to believe it was imminent. Something always seemed to be missing for me—mutual respect, ability to communicate, availability—it was always something.

Jim loved to talk about his ranch and his days on the bench. Sometimes it felt as if he was just processing his memories out loud and I happened to be within hearing range.

"Sentenced a kid once to help out at his church fur a month," he said as we headed into day five of the project.

Only in Texas, I thought.

"Doubt it was my best decision. Don't know if it made any lasting change in that kid, but his mama su'gested it after he stole money from one a her church ladies. Nice-lookin' kid…real smart. Wish I knew what happened to 'im…if he made his mama proud or went south on 'er."

We kept screwing lattice across the patio cover. Bonnie had decided to grow queen's wreath vine across the top, and we wanted to be sure the quality of the structure complemented the flora.

"So what're you plannin' ta do once your daughter goes off ta college?" Jim asked as we continued attaching the lattice.

"Keep working," I said.

"Why?"

"Well, I can't afford to retire yet, and I like my work."

"Good reasons," Jim said. "But not good enough."

"What are you asking?"

"I'm asking how you're goin' ta go from a day-to-day dad to 'n empty house without losin' your reason ta git up in the mornin'."

"That's an odd question, Jim. I don't feel I'm at risk for empty-nest syndrome, do you?"

Jim chuckled. "Not empty nest. Maybe empty heart."

I stopped the power drill and looked at him. "Empty heart?"

"Ah, lemme stop makin' you guess an' jus' tell ya. When Emma died, I'd jus' retired from judgin' and was plannin' ta work m' ranch. I didn't think much about workin' 'cause Emma and me, we had each other and the ranch we both loved. It jus' made sense ta git up in the mornin' an' go work. Then we come out here fur a visit two years 'go, an' the accident happened and suddenly nothin' seemed ta matter anymore. Went back ta my ranch fur a while but didn't know why I was gettin' up and workin' so hard when there was no one ta come home to. I guess what I'm sayin' is…have you decided what your life is goin' to look like when your lil' gal leaves for college?"

190

"Well," I said, "I'll be working for another four years of college tuition payments."

"Yeah, four if you're lucky, but I'm pritty sure ya don't have ta work sixty hours a week fur that."

"No."

"That all ya want your life and work to count for, Mike? College tuition?"

I wasn't sure how to answer that. "I'm not sure, Jim. It's not a bad thing."

"No, it ain't. It's a good thing fur your kids."

"But if you're asking what legacy I'm leaving, or what larger purpose my life has, I can't answer that because I've never really thought about it. All I ever thought I was supposed to do is provide for my family and be a decent guy."

"Well, ya are that, son. Definitely a good provider an' decent guy..." Jim paused. "But ya could be more."

I didn't say anything for a minute or two as we went back to the latticework.

"They say," Jim began again, "the basic questions a' life are who am I, where am I goin', an' how did I get here."

"Have you answered those for yourself?" I asked.

"B'lieve I have. A few times."

"So it doesn't have to be a final answer?"

"Nothin' is final on this ole planet 'cept death."

"Will you share your answers?" I asked.

"Wouldn't 'ave brought up the subject 'less I was willin', but I'm not share'n mine till ya figure out yours first."

I nodded. No decent judge would allow conclusion without consideration.

"Let me think about it," I said. "It's something worth thinking about."

I thought about those questions a lot the next week as we drove to Tahoe. Both kids were engrossed in their videos or computers, and I had many hours of silence to consider what my life would look like after they were independent adults. I had never pictured myself as anything but a married man when my children left home. It would be my wife and me waving good-bye to our youngest and returning home to the romance of

191

an empty house. In the process of providing a stable post-divorce home for my kids, I had neglected to plan for the day they would leave. Now it was just eighteen months away. My purpose in life had to be larger than just Provider Dad, or someday I would become obsolete.

40

FEBRUARY

I couldn't really answer who I was. So I hit Stuart with that question during our session in February. I'd seen people pondering a lot of personal questions as the twentieth century ended. With predictions of world's end and terrible calamity, suddenly it was popular to self-evaluate. I had no interest in self-evaluation then, and I thought most of the cataclysmic predictions were hype anyway...just reasons to reel in the gullible.

"A friend and I have been talking about the big questions of life, Stuart."

"And those would be...?"

"Who am I? How did I get here? Where am I going?"

"Valuable questions to explore."

"So how do you begin answering those? I know I'm an attorney and I should know how to dig into it, but all I keep coming up with is: I'm an attorney, the son of Art and Irene Passick, the ex-husband of Dayne, the father of Matt and MarLea, and the partner of Rob."

"So you define yourself solely by other people's relation to you?"

"Usually."

"And how do you address the question of how did I get here?"

"I don't."

"Well then," Stuart said, "that gives us a good place to start today."

"Maybe I should just avoid the deep questions and face what's in front of me."

"A lot of people do that, but I don't think it's the best approach. It's a reactive approach."

"Most of my life has been reactive, Stuart. At least when it comes to relationships. People do something and I react or retreat."

"Is that what you want your life to be, Mike? A life of react or retreat?"

"No."

"Then how are you going to change that?"

"By answering the first question. Deciding who I am."

We spent the next thirty minutes exploring ways people defined themselves, and I realized something profound. I had no bloodlines or social status to define me. I'd been raised with no spiritual beliefs and had developed none of my own. I had no passion for volunteerism or civic projects. After a full exploration, I realized I defined myself only as a man, an attorney, a decent golfer, and a father. Nothing more.

"Does that feel like enough for you, Mike?"

"Should it?"

"That's a personal decision."

"No, it doesn't."

"Then you may want to explore additional ways of defining yourself, deciding who you are in this world," Stuart said as our session ended. "Ways that feel more complete."

But where do I start? That thought bounced around my brain as I drove. Rob would probably talk about it with his small group, but I didn't have a small group. Well, technically I didn't, but maybe in reality I did. I had Rob and Jim and, of course, Stuart. Except for Stuart, I didn't meet regularly with these guys, and the four of us didn't sit in one room together every week. But they were my friends and in some ways my accountability group. They were the men I trusted and whose opinions I valued. I knew Jim wouldn't share his answers with me yet, but Rob might. It was worth a shot.

I found Rob sitting in his office the next morning.

"You busy?"

"Sort of," Rob said. "What's up?"

"This may sound a little too touchy-feely, but I have a question."

Rob put down the pen in his hand and looked at me. "Sounds deep."

"It is. I realized yesterday that I don't really know who I am or how I fit into the larger scheme of life."

"Wow, that is deep," Rob said.

"Ever since I was a kid, I've subconsciously defined myself by what I'm not. I'm not the bully my father was, I'm not an escape artist like my brother. And since Dayne left, I'm not a husband. When I ask myself who I am, all I can come up with is a man, an attorney, a golfer, and a dad—and a bunch of things I'm not."

Rob nodded.

"Any idea why?" I asked.

Rob thought for a moment. "Well," he said, "I have a theory."

"OK," I said.

"There's no broad perspective, no larger view. Your definition has no spiritual or community element to it. You didn't even mention you're a friend. You are a friend to Leanne and me and probably a lot of other people."

"That's because I'm not sure I've been much of a friend. When was the last time I had you guys over? When was the last time I did anything for you?"

"Maybe you need to reexamine your definition of friendship," Rob said. "It's not about what you do for me. It's about our connection with each other." He paused. "That is an interesting point though. Notice most of your definitions of yourself require you to do something. Your definition of yourself always comes from your own effort. Don't you think you have some inherent value just because you're Mike Passick?"

"Not really. Do you?"

"Well." Rob paused. "As a Christian, I define myself first as a child of God. That's where I start."

"I realized yesterday I really don't have any context like that from either my childhood or my adult life."

"Spirituality doesn't always take the forefront when we start defining ourselves in college and young adulthood," Rob said. "Believe me, I know. It took me years of exploration and decisions to finally determine what I believe and why."

"So does having that spiritual context make that much difference for you?"

"It defines everything I do. It gives a broader context to the way I treat other people, not just for my own ego, but for larger, more important reasons."

"I don't know that I treat people nicely for my own ego."

"I wasn't insinuating you do. I just said my motivation in college was more ego driven than altruistic."

"Got it. Is that spiritual-community context the reason you and Leanne volunteer at that shelter?"

"One of the main reasons."

"Interesting," I said as I stood up. "Hey, I don't want to take up too much time this morning, but I was just wondering."

"Mike," Rob said as I walked out of his office.

"Yeah?"

"Don't be too hard on yourself. You're a lot more than you give yourself credit for."

"Thanks, buddy," I said. "Appreciate that." I knew he meant it. Rob wasn't one to lie. But I wondered if I believed it.

41

OCTOBER

Bonnie called early one morning. The clock said six, and I wasn't fully awake yet.

"Mike, I'm sorry to bother you so early. I just wanted you to know that my dad fell this morning, and I'm in emergency with him. He probably needs stitches and might have a concussion, but he's not seriously hurt."

Suddenly I was wide awake.

"I'll be right there."

"Mike, we're fine. You don't have to come. It's early. I'm sure you have things to do today."

"I'll be right there, Bonnie. What hospital?"

"Saddleback."

When I arrived, Jim was sitting next to Bonnie in the waiting area, an ice pack against his right temple.

"Dang rug," Jim said.

"You'll do anything to get some attention, won't you?" I said as I sat down.

"That's right," Jim said without looking directly at me. "Gotta' do somethin' ta keep this little gal's attention."

Bonnie smiled her well-practiced smile. She looked exhausted.

"Have you eaten anything?" I asked her.

"Not yet."

197

"Want me to get something for you? I'm sure there's a cafeteria somewhere in here."

"Actually, would you mind sitting with dad while I went for a cup of coffee and some yogurt? Dad, you want me to bring something back for you?"

"Just a cuppa coffee," Jim said. "Doubt they'd let ya bring bacon an' eggs in here."

"Probably not," Bonnie said as she stood up. "Thanks, Mike. I'll be right back."

Jim and I sat in silence for a few minutes as televisions pumped out the morning news and traffic reports. A family of four sat under one of the windows. A sleepy little boy tried to get his mother's attention as she attempted to comfort a crying baby. The father kept halfheartedly reaching for the little boy's pajama sleeve, but the child adeptly stayed just out of reach. It'll always feel like that, I thought to myself. Your son will always feel just out of reach. I missed Jim's commentary on the parents and their kids, but I realized he was probably not in the mood to notice other people right now.

"Do you have a headache?" I asked.

"Yup," he said. "Mostly from just sittin' here waitin'. Too much noise." His voice was flat and tired, completely void of its usual spark.

I looked up to see Bonnie walking toward us. "Here, Dad," she said, handing him a coffee cup. "I'm so sorry, Mike. I didn't even think to ask if you wanted anything. Forgive me."

"That's OK," I said. "I'll catch something on the way back home."

"I'm really sorry."

I sat quietly for a few seconds while Bonnie settled into her seat. It felt strange to have Bonnie apologize for such a small thing. In fact, it felt odd to have her apologize to me at all. She'd thanked me for coming to help her and apologized for not getting me coffee—all within thirty minutes. I was pretty sure I hadn't heard either of those things from Dayne in over nineteen years of marriage. I was beginning to find Bonnie intriguing. Although she was sad, she was still considerate. Although she'd lost her husband and mother, she was still kind. She consistently showed tenderness toward both Jim and me. Somehow that morning I realized these traits were as attractive to me as her long legs and toned figure.

A nurse called Jim's name.

"I'll wait here," I said to Bonnie as she stood. "I have some calls to make."

"We're OK," Bonnie said. "Really, we're fine. You can go. I'll call you when we get home and let you know how he's doing."

"You sure?"

"Yes, we're fine."

"OK, call me when you get back home."

"I will," Bonnie said. "Thanks so much, Mike. It was good to have you here." She turned toward me, gave me a tight hug, and then walked with her dad into the treatment area.

"Thanks, son," Jim said, turning toward me just before the door closed. "'Preciate it." His voice was more subdued than usual.

Bonnie called at ten. "We're back home and dad's resting in his chair."

"What'd they decide?"

"He has a slight concussion and needed a few stitches, but nothing too serious. I was concerned because the cut was deep and he seemed a little disoriented when I found him."

"So what happened?"

"This loud noise woke me up about four fifteen. Apparently Dad got up to go to the bathroom and slipped on the bathroom rug. He went down hard and hit his head on the edge of the sink. Fortunately, a plastic surgeon was at the hospital and did a beautiful job sewing him up. Dad was worried about a big scar."

"Who would have thought a Texas rancher would worry about a scar?" I said.

"Dad was always particular about his appearance, even before he became a judge," Bonnie said. "I think he was so awed by my mother's beauty that he made it a point to look as good as he could. Anyway, he's just supposed to take it easy and see the doctor again in ten days."

"Good news. I'm glad to hear he wasn't more seriously hurt."

"Me too."

"Thanks for calling, Bonnie. I'd better get back to work."

"Hey, Mike," she said. "Would you and MarLea like to come over for dinner tonight? I think Dad would enjoy some company."

"MarLea has a review session tonight and won't be home until eight. But I'd enjoy dinner if the invitation can be adjusted to one."

"Of course," Bonnie said. "I forgot about that review session. Brandon's there too, and I think the kids are just grabbing burgers between that and afternoon practice. Can you come around six? It'll be the three of us."

"Sure," I said. "See you then. Tell Jim I'm glad he's OK."

Bonnie had fish tacos on the table when I arrived.

"I heard your car," she said as we walked into the dining room. "Dad's hungry, so let's eat."

Jim was already sitting at the head of the table, so Bonnie and I took our places on the two sides. As I passed the food, I realized how familial it felt at this table. Conversation appeared without effort. There was no tension, no harsh words, no walking on eggshells. Just good food. Someone driving by the window would assume we were all related, but they'd have no idea we were related by friendship and grief. They'd think we were a family.

I helped Bonnie with the dishes as Jim walked slowly to his chair in the living room and clicked on the TV.

"Dad's being hard on himself for falling," Bonnie said.

"Most men would be."

"I know, but I hate to see him beat himself up over something so small."

"Want me to talk to him? Don't know if it'll make any difference, but I can try."

"Yeah," she said, "if he wants to talk. I think he's pretty tired, so he may go to bed soon."

"Are you supposed to check on him during the night? Because of the concussion?"

"They didn't say I had to, but I'll probably get up a couple of times tonight. He's not young anymore, and I want to be sure he's OK."

I kept loading the dishwasher as Bonnie rinsed dishes and wiped the countertops.

"Go ahead," she said. "I'll finish up."

I walked into the living room and sat down. Jim turned the TV off but didn't look directly at me.

"How are you feeling?" I asked.

"Like a dang idiot," he said.

"Really? Why?"

"Didn't 'spect I'd be sittin' in a hospital with my daughter at six in the mornin' cause I fell on a bathroom rug. Thought I might have a heart 'tack or somethin' serious someday, but didn't 'spect ta trip on a damn bathroom rug."

I thought about saying "Don't be so hard on yourself" or "Everyone falls sometime" but decided to skip the platitudes and avoid minimizing his frustration. I knew I'd feel the same way if I were in his position, and Jim had earned the right to show honest emotion around me.

"I heard you have a concussion," I said. "Is the headache still bad?"

"It was," he said. "Doc gave me some pain meds ta take the edge off. I prob'ly need another dose 'bout now."

He rose and walked slowly to the kitchen. I heard Bonnie shake a container then pour liquid into a glass.

"Forgive me, son," Jim said, standing at the kitchen door. "I'm feelin' a lil' tir'd, so I'm headed up ta bed. Think ya could drop by tomorra 'r the next day? Might be up fur conversation by then."

"Sure, Jim," I said. "I'll see you in a couple of days."

Bonnie watched her dad walk to his room and then turned to me.

"I guess I should go," I said. "The kids will be done soon."

"Actually," Bonnie said, "it's only a little before seven. Would you like to have dessert on the patio?"

I helped her arrange brownies at the bottom of two bowls and then top them with ice cream and a spoonful of hot fudge. We walked outside and settled into lawn chairs as the sun dropped low on the horizon. The breeze was cool and trees danced to the song of twilight as we ate. Above us songbirds settled onto their nighttime branches and individual clouds joined together to form the evening's coastal fog.

"Would you like a jacket?" Bonnie asked as she stood and gathered our bowls. "I'm going to grab one. The ice cream made me chilly."

"Thanks, I'm good," I said.

I sat watching the birds and trees while Bonnie went in. Her backyard was compact but pretty, with geraniums in flower pots and a small herb garden at one end of the covered patio. I was looking at the little garden when she returned.

"I like fresh herbs," she said. "My husband was a terrific gardener. We always had fresh vegetables and fruit, but I can't seem to find the motivation to plant more than herbs these days."

I nodded.

"I keep wondering when I'll stop thinking about him every day," she said. "When will I see tomatoes or Corvettes or a football game and not think of Rich?"

I had no answer, so I just looked at her in silence.

"Do you miss Dayne like that?" she asked. "I know divorce isn't the same, but do you miss her?"

I thought for a moment. If I told her my real feelings about Dayne, I would sound pathetic and self-serving, so I searched my memory for something I truly missed.

"I miss our good days together. Cuddling by the fire when we were first married, walking hand in hand through the neighborhood when our kids were young."

Bonnie nodded.

"But divorce is different. Especially the circumstances of my divorce. So truthfully, I try not to think about her much. I focus on the kids and work."

"I sometimes wish I had work to escape to," Bonnie said. "Before the accident, I was an operating room nurse."

"Really? You never mentioned that."

"It seems like a lifetime ago," she said sadly. "When Mom and Rich died, everything changed. After a few months of living in different states, Dad and I decided we needed to live together, so he sold his ranch, paid off my house, and set up a trust fund for Brandon and me. I might go back to work after Brandon leaves for college, because I enjoyed my work, but I won't if Dad needs a lot of care. He's been there for me, so I want to be there for him."

"Do you think he'll be all right tomorrow?"

"Oh yeah. He's a strong man, still very healthy for his age. So this won't keep him down long unless he starts really missing Mom again."

"I'll try to come over in a couple of days to distract him," I said.

"That would be great." Bonnie smiled at me.

"Bonnie," I said, gathering my courage, "I always enjoy the time I spend with you and your dad."

"We do too," she said.

202

"Do you think you and I might be heading in a direction that's more than friendship?"

"What makes you ask that, Mike?" she said softly.

"I've been around for a while now, and I've noticed you're a beautiful woman inside and out. You care so deeply for people, and you have such a kind heart. Nice legs too. You're more and more attractive to me the longer I know you."

Bonnie blushed, although I had to look closely to tell. The sun had disappeared, and the lights inside the house created backlighting on the patio.

"Oh, Mike," she said. "I've thought about this so many times. You're one of the most attractive, nicest men I know. I love being near you and always enjoy when you come over." I realized her words didn't seem to be leading to a passionate kiss, but rather than jump to a hasty conclusion, I listened quietly. "I've dreamt about you. I always look forward to seeing you. I thought throughout the summer that maybe it was our destiny to be together." She stopped looking at me for a moment and looked at one of her geraniums. The light from the kitchen reflected off the top of her hair and her cheekbone. She was like a Rembrandt painting, shadows everywhere except for touches of light at key focal points. I wished those points would give me a glimpse into her eyes, but only her cheek and hair grabbed the scarce particles of light.

"I've thought about it. I've prayed about it. I've even talked to one of my closest friends about it. But, ultimately I have to face reality. The man I still want to walk through the door and kiss me is Rich. I still miss him every moment of every day. I still long for his touch and keep his sweatshirt in my drawer so I can remember the smell of his skin. I reach for him in the night, and I'm still shocked that he's not there."

My heart sank. There's no competing with a dead man. If she just needed time, I could give her that. If she wasn't sure about my motives or the details of my failed marriage, I could reassure her. But I couldn't replace Rich, the father of her son, the man who still monopolized her heart.

"I understand," I said.

"I hope you do, because I don't." Her voice broke. "It's been two years. He's dead. He'll never walk through the door again or lay next to me at night when I need someone to comfort me."

I reached for her hand, and she didn't draw away.

"Oh, Mike, I wanted to love you that much. I know you're a man who would make me happy and provide a wonderful example to Brandon." She wiped a tear with the back of her hand. "But I can't stop loving Rich. I don't know how to stop loving him."

"Bonnie," I said, her hand still holding mine, "I may not fully understand, but I admire you. I wish I could say I've loved someone that much... enough to make them irreplaceable. I don't understand that love because I've never experienced it. Maybe someday I'll be lucky enough to, but it hasn't happened for me yet." I paused to organize my thoughts, which were traveling like an explosion in all directions. "We have a wonderful, comfortable friendship, and I'm happy to keep it that way."

"Me too," she said in almost a whisper. "Please don't stop coming over."

"I won't. You and Jim are an important part of my life. I'm not ready to lose that, plus I'd probably starve if it weren't for you."

Bonnie laughed as she wiped an errant tear.

"I'd better go," I said. "MarLea will be home soon."

"OK."

Bonnie stood up. "After all that, would it be inappropriate to give you a hug?" she asked.

"Hugs are always appreciated," I said. "Remember, we're supposed to need four a day."

"Yeah, I'm a little low right now."

"Me too," I said, wrapping her in my arms. "You're a wonderful friend, Bonnie. Thanks for being honest with me."

"I couldn't lie to you, Mike. You mean too much to me."

42

MARLEA'S SENIOR YEAR

Jim healed without a scar, Bonnie kept her scars hidden behind smiles and plates of incredibly satisfying food, and I tried to get past the feeling I would never know true love in this lifetime. If there's an afterlife, I hoped it would include pure, honest, unadulterated love so I could finally experience it. Maybe I needed to get a dog.

MarLea studied with Brandon, Connor, and Kate as soon as school began again. Then suddenly MarLea and Brandon announced they were dating in late September. He was a nice kid, so I had no reservations. Bonnie and I agreed they could hang out at either house as long as a parent was home. That meant they were with Bonnie and Jim in the late afternoons, so I would often get a call around four thirty inviting me for dinner. Things were never uncomfortable between Bonnie and me. We just kept being friends, and I instructed my brain to view her as nothing more than the mom of MarLea's boyfriend. I'm not sure why, but it worked. Gradually my feelings of attraction retreated.

I'd spent most of the year talking with Stuart about my self-image and how my childhood and marriage had colored that view. Apparently over the years I developed quite a talent for boxing up my own view of myself and allowing others to define me, often in ways that were skewed. Stuart helped me strip away the untruths spattered across my self-image

205

and replace them with a clearer view. Gradually, when I listened to the voice in my head, it didn't sound so much like my father's or Dayne's. It stopped being my harshest critic.

"So have you answered who am I yet?" Stuart asked me one afternoon in late September.

"Getting there," I said.

"So?"

"I'm a man who believes in living life by my values. The people I care about can rely on me to help and follow through on my promises. I show up and do the things that need to be done. I'm not always perfect and I make mistakes, but in general I'm a man of honor."

"That's a nice start," Stuart said. "It beats your previous definition because it can reach across all the areas of your life...being a father, an attorney, a son, maybe a husband and volunteer someday. If I remember right, you said you'd like to have some community involvement once the kids leave home. This definition isn't dependent on your relationship to them or anyone else. It's about the core of you."

"It took a while to figure out, but it feels right to me. I'm happy with the answer to that question."

"Have you tackled the other two?"

"Not yet," I said. "To answer how did I get here, I have to take a look into spirituality and science. To see what I really believe about the origin of things and how life came to be on this planet."

"Are you saying you have to decide if there's a God to answer that question?"

"Yeah," I said. "I think I do. I need to decide that for myself rather than just ignoring it or believing by default."

"Sounds like a good plan," Stuart said. "Let me know where your search leads you."

I called Jim on the way home. "Doing anything important tonight?" I asked.

"Just sittin' here lis'nin' to some weather guy take a stab at predictin' California weather," he said. "It ain't Texas that's for sure."

"Want to make a Target run with me?"

"Sure. When'll you be here?"

"About ten minutes."

"Be waitin' on the porch."

Jim and I headed for Target, avoiding the bicycles with too few lights and the joggers in dark clothes. "I wouldn't convict the driver who hit 'em," Jim said. "Ya can't see 'em. You'd think they'd be a lil' smarter 'bout what they wear an' get a reflector or two on them bikes."

After we finished shopping and looking at the latest electronics, we headed back toward Bonnie's house.

"So are you ready to share your answers to the big questions with me?" I asked.

"Decided for y'urself yet?"

"I'm getting there. I've decided who I am right now...maybe not next month or six years from now, but right now. I'm a man of values who does the honorable thing most of the time. I'm someone who's there when people need me."

"Not too bad," Jim said. "That's a good start."

"So who are you?"

"I'm a man who tries to find the balance between justice and grace, and I put my family first."

"I like it."

"Don't mean ta be disrespectful, son, but it don't matter if ya like it. These'r my answers not yours."

I nodded and pulled over to the curb. "Have you figured out how you got here and where you're going?"

"Have you?" Jim asked. "Ya really want my answers 'fore you've determined 'em for yourself?"

"Yeah, I think I do."

"Why?"

"Because," I said, "you're the closest thing to a good father I've ever known. I value your opinion as a judge and as a friend, and I think you have some wisdom I need to hear."

"That's a tall order, son," Jim said, shaking his head. "Don't know if I deserve that praise, but seein' as how your dad didn't set much of 'n example, guess I c'n share my thoughts." He paused and looked out the window at the streetlights reflecting off the pavement. The coastal fog began to spread its fingers through the neighborhood, and little bits of moisture clung to the windows of my car.

"Long tima'go, 'bout the time Emma and I married, I d'cided I might become a dad someday. Seemed foolish ta tell a child things ya don't believe yourself, so I started lookin' into what I b'lieved and why. Read lotsa books, listened ta lotsa so-called experts. After all that, I's more confused than before. Try'n to d'cide where I was goin' was jus' 'nother way of askin' what I was doin' with my life and whether there was anything ta look forward ta aft'ward. I decided ta let the question of how I got here lie still for a while and focus on where I was goin'.

"I couldn't talk to Emma 'bout that, 'cause she's the daughter of a Baptist preacher and she never once questioned her comin' into this world or where she was goin' when she left it, but I's more skeptic'l. So I started thinkin' about it night after night. One night after I'd been workin' the ranch all day and still had ta go out an' find a missin' steer, I was thinkin' 'bout it again. Looked up in that bright Texas sky and saw all them stars and planets and such, and jus' decided then and there that all of us livin' on this planet and breathin' and lovin' each other and all, among all them stars and planets, it jus' couldn't 've happened by accident.

"I don't claim to know Emma's God the way she did, but I've decided he's prob'ly out there, and if he was kind 'nough ta give me Emma then he mus' be generous. An' if he b'lieves in accountability so as ta let me feel the cons'quences of m' own bad choices, then he must have a strong sense a justice. Felt ta me like there mus' be a reason for existin' that's bigger than m' own comfort. I know it ain't the most logical argument anyone ever put t'gether, but it made sense ta me and, for unknown reasons, still does. I d'cided I want m' life to be built 'round that idea...that if you're the big guy on the block, God or the president or just a scrawny li'l local judge, you ough'a think every day about the confluence a justice and grace—being fair and being kind, but not lettin' too many things slide by. Lookin' at the bigger picture before ya hand down decisions or judgments. I decided I'd like ta meet God someday. Hopefully I'll get the chance.

"I don't know if that entirely answers the question of where I'm goin', but it feels complete ta me." He paused for a moment. "As to them li'l details of how we got here, I don't much care."

I burst out laughing. "Seriously?"

"Yeah, that's why I didn't wanna tell ya. 'Cause I just don't care. I'm here and I'm living what I b'lieve to be the best life I can. I talk ta God

208

every day, but I ain't never heard him talk back, so I trust if there's an after-life and Emma's there, she won't let me go nowhere else. That's how I deal with them hard questions."

After I dropped Jim off, I realized his answers didn't fully satisfy me. But perhaps that was the point of the questions. To force each of us to answer for ourselves because no one else's answers could possibly feel like the right fit. Like my choice of a spouse, a profession, and a million other daily life choices, those answers had to be mine and mine alone.

43

OCTOBER, A FEW DAYS AFTER WHAT WOULD HAVE BEEN OUR TWENTY-SECOND ANNIVERSARY

I was sitting home reading a contract and listening to Seal belt out "It's a Man's World" when I remembered Brooke's Christmas card. I'd never called her. She'd sent one or two greetings through Carol, but I'd just said, "Tell her I said hi." Somehow it seemed important to reach out to her this particular night, so I picked up the phone and dialed her number.

"Hello there, Mike," she said after the second ring. "I wondered if you'd fallen off the planet."

"Not quite," I said. "Just busy trying to stay ahead of work and a high school senior who is dating."

"Dating?"

"Yes, she's almost eighteen now."

"Wow, time flies."

"It does and we haven't been very good about keeping in touch, have we?"

"I wasn't sure you wanted to talk after what I pulled in that restaurant."

"You didn't pull anything, Brooke. You just said what you felt, and you were right. We both had healing to do."

"Yes, but I could have been a little more gentle, a little more...oh... kind, I guess."

"Maybe just a little," I said.

"Is it too late to apologize?"

"I don't think apologies have an expiration date, but it's not necessary," I said. "If I'd held any grudge, I wouldn't have called you."

"You didn't call for a long time."

"I didn't know if you wanted to talk to me."

"OK, fair enough," she said. "So can we attempt to forget my odd behavior?"

"Only if you stop being so hard on yourself. What you did was speak hard truth, not exhibit odd behavior. You didn't start an audience sing-along dressed as a Disney princess."

Brooke laughed. A beautiful laugh. A familiar laugh that sounded like something I could happily hear every day for the rest of my life.

"When are you coming to California again?" I asked.

"How soon can you pick me up?"

"Ten minutes."

"I'll start packing now."

We talked for over an hour, sharing stories from our lives, and ultimately decided to talk again soon. I called her the next day. This time we talked about the big questions of life, and I was fascinated to discover Brooke, like me, had just begun exploring those for herself.

"It's impossible to be a better person making better choices if I'm not willing to peel away the layers of dysfunction and avoidance that keep leading me to unavailable men," she said that night. "I'm trying to figure out who I am and who I want to be. It's an interesting journey. Glad I have a good therapist and some great friends."

We spent three hours on the phone that night, and it didn't seem long enough.

Brooke and I talked on the phone every night for over two months. We texted during the day, flirting and teasing. I started to feel alive again. Finally, one bright December afternoon, she stood on the curb at the airport waiting for me. I drove up with the clear memory of the first time I saw her standing at the same curb, beside the same recycling container, shielding her eyes with the same hand.

I hustled to get her bags in the trunk and give her a quick hug before airport security shooed me away like an unwanted pest. As soon as I passed the airport exit, I pulled into a bank parking lot. Brooke looked at me quizically. I threw open my door and headed straight for her side of the car.

"Brooke," I said, holding out my hand to her as she smiled at me from the front seat, "let's do this right." It took an instant for her to swing her legs out of the car and reach for me. The strength of her hug surprised me, but I realized for probably the first time in our relationship, neither of us was holding back. It was probably our first unreserved hug, and it melded into a long passionate kiss.

"I've waited a long time for that kiss," Brooke said.

"Too long," I said, kissing her again.

I'd arranged for Brooke to meet my kids at dinner that evening. Matt was home for the holidays. I'd told them Brooke was Carol's niece and I thought she might be someone special in my life. Like most kids their age, Matt and MarLea had other things on their minds, but they were interested to meet her.

"We have some time before dinner," I said to her as we drove. "Would you like to drop by my house, or should I take you directly to Carol's?"

"I'd like to see my aunt, but truthfully, I'd love to see your house. You know, I've never seen it."

"Wow, that's right," I said. "The kids are out with friends and will meet us at the restaurant, so I have time to give you the grand tour before dinner." We walked through the front door and stood in the entry for a few moments while Brooke scanned the living room, dining room, staircase, and the door to my study.

"It's beautiful. There's still a distinctive woman's touch here."

"Yeah," I said. "I haven't changed the living room or dining room since Dayne left. Those rooms were always her domain. I had no influence there, so I just left them."

213

"Did she take the painting or whatever was over the fireplace?"

"No, actually she didn't. I just disposed of that painting myself a few weeks ago."

Brooke's eyes sparkled with curiosity. "Disposed of it?"

I nodded. "Would you like to hear that tale of destruction?"

"Definitely."

I poured us both an Arnold Palmer and led the way through the back door to the chairs on the patio.

"This view is amazing, Mike," Brooke said, lacing her fingers in mine. "I'd be out here all the time if I lived with this view."

"It is beautiful," I said. "But only if things in the house are happy. Otherwise it's a waste of money."

We stood looking out over the Pacific for a few minutes, our hands and sides touching as the sun sprinkled warmth across our faces. I watched Brooke as she scanned the horizon. Catalina was barely visible, and when she finally saw it, the delight spread across her face and settled into a single dimple. I couldn't take my eyes off her happiness. It felt to me as though the entire house breathed a sigh of relief.

"So," Brooke said teasingly, "tell me about your penchant for destroying fine art."

"It's a long story."

"We have a bit of time before dinner."

"Well," I said, "let me give you something to read first." I walked into my study and gathered the page I'd written.

"Should I read this now?"

"Please."

Brooke sat in silence. I watched concentration deepen as she read the first sentences:

They say you marry your unfinished business. If that is true—and from my experience it must be—then I walked down a path created by my father and fell over a cliff into the arms of my wife...

When she finished reading the entire page, she laid it on her lap and looked at me. "That's very well written, Mike. I assume the family portrait used to hang over the fireplace?"

"Yes," I said. "Until three weeks ago."

Brooke reached for my hand.

214

"Three weeks ago, I came home one night and realized I didn't want that picture in my house anymore. Not only did it represent the life I was trying to move beyond, but it was a visual representation of all the lies I'd been forced to live: the lie that we had a happy family, the lie that we were a cohesive husband-and-wife team, the lie that passion lingered nearby. And suddenly, I couldn't stand the idea of that stupid portrait being on the wall anymore.

"I knew Dayne didn't care about it, or she would have taken it. So I picked up the phone and called Matt. He said he'd always hated it, from the moment he saw it. To him it was fiction then and fiction now. So then I had to talk with MarLea. My sweet, tenderhearted MarLea."

Brooke listened intently as she gazed out over the ocean.

"I waited until she came home from studying at Brandon's house. She looked so beautiful walking through the door that night, her long hair pulled back and her backpack slung over her shoulder. She and I talked about the photo for over an hour, remembering the tension between Dayne and the photographer over little details. MarLea remembered the day we hung it over the fireplace and how the evening had ended with Dayne angry at me. I didn't even remember that. Finally, I asked MarLea if she wanted to keep the picture, and all she said was, 'Why? Do whatever you want with it, Dad. I don't have any fond memories attached to that picture. It just makes me sad.'

"So the next afternoon, when I was home by myself, I took my utility knife and cut it out of the frame. Then I rolled it up and went to stuff it in the garbage. But here's where it gets funny, Brooke. It didn't feel right to just put it out with the trash to decompose in the county dump."

Brooke stopped looking at the horizon and turned toward me. "So what did you do with it?" she asked.

"I found this old metal trash can in the side yard...one of those trash cans we all had before cities provided new ones...and I put it in there."

Brooke smiled, knowing there was more to the story. "And..."

"Then I remembered this bottle of Cognac I'd bought years ago thinking Dayne and I would drink it on our twentieth anniversary. I poured myself a glass, and as I was sipping it, watching the sunset, I realized alcohol and canvas burn very nicely."

"You didn't!" Brooke exclaimed.

"No, I didn't. I drank the Cognac and doused the portrait with lighter fluid. Then I lit it and watched it burn."

"You're lucky some neighbor didn't report you," Brooke said with a laugh.

"Probably."

"Did it feel good?"

"Oh, I don't know if I'd call it *good*. It felt like an ending, but it still doesn't feel done."

"Why?"

"I don't know."

Brooke and I sat there thinking our own thoughts for a minute. I realized again that it didn't feel done. It felt as if I'd burned my former life of lies, but it wasn't buried.

"Hey," Brooke said suddenly. "Do you want to go for a drive?"

"Right now?"

"Yeah, before dinner."

"OK."

"Come with me first," she said, reaching for my hand. "Do you have a jar or a plastic container?"

I went into the house and came back with a plastic container I used for leftovers. "You're not planning on putting anything of importance in this, are you?"

"Depends how you define *importance*," she said as she walked toward the side yard. Together we looked into the metal trash can. There was a pile of ashes and a few pieces of canvas.

"I take it we're going to dispose of these," I said.

"Yes," Brooke said. "You said it felt burned but not buried. Instead of burying it, why don't we scatter these ashes?"

We somehow managed to pour the majority of the ashes into the container, and then we drove out to a favorite spot of mine that overlooked the ocean and was far from the crowds. The afternoon sun reflected off the small waves that broke in a smooth white line. A gentle breeze tenderly brushed Brooke's hair away from her face and made it curl around the edges of her chin.

216

"Do you want to say a few words before we scatter the ashes, Reverend Mike?"

We both laughed.

"Here," Brooke said as she handed the container to me. "Just be sure to stand upwind."

I stood there for a moment holding the ashes of our family portrait. It had seemed so much easier to burn it than to stand here and scatter it to the wind. Burning it was my act of defiance. Scattering these ashes was a tacit admission that we were each going our own way. In spite of the fact we all stood together in one picture at a time in the past, we each had to decide the big questions of the future for ourselves.

I stood quietly for a moment, my arm around Brooke's shoulders, and then I released the ashes and watched them choose whether to rise or fall. Some grabbed the wind and soared upward. Others dropped to the ground without any effort.

"Thank you for doing this with me," I said after an appropriate amount of silence. "Somehow releasing the ashes felt more fitting than just throwing them in the trash."

"All those years together deserve better than the city dump," she said quietly. She reached for my hand as we walked back to the car. The sun was low on the horizon, enticing us to linger, so we leaned against the fender and watched as the sun winked good-bye to her audience—tourists and locals watching the day's twilight performance.

"You know, Brooke," I said, "I've been thinking about some of life's big questions. I have this desire to dig deeper and figure things out... to explore who I am and who I want to be. And I don't want to do it alone." I squeezed her hand and pulled her close. "Thanks for understanding my need to burn that family portrait and give it a proper send-off. I feel like right now I'm on a journey to let some things go and hold on to others, to answer the bigger questions I never wanted to deal with before."

"I get that," she said. "I have more questions than answers right now too. Maybe that's just a sign we're open to learning. Maybe all these difficulties have made us more...I don't know...more...willing to consider a different approach to life. A healthier approach."

"I know one thing for sure," I said. "Little by little, I'm starting to understand the effect my father's and my wife's words have had on me. They've left scars where memories should be. Little by little I'm discovering why I enjoy being around you—why we belong together. It's because I long to be with someone who actually wants to be with me."

"I get that," Brooke said as she touched my face. "I like the idea of us together. I love being with you, and when we're apart, I miss you."

"I miss you too. Life feels more complete when we're together. Now, let's see if you pass the 'kid test,'" I said, smiling.

"Are you worried?"

"Not at all," I said. "They're going to like you a lot."

Suddenly, I couldn't wait to introduce Brooke to Matt and MarLea. I felt good about the new direction my life was taking. I knew what belonged in my future and I knew what needed to stay behind. For the first time in years, I allowed myself to think that maybe, just maybe, I might have a chance at the deep, rich experience of loving someone who chose to love me too. What would it be like to love a woman who wasn't looking for all the ways I could disappoint or anger her?

Darkness settled over the vast expanse of the Pacific Ocean, and house lights began to decorate the hills. Dark on one side, light on the other. Such a contrast. I reached across the console and held Brooke's hand as we drove north on Pacific Coast Highway to meet my kids for dinner.

"If you want to become healthy, you have to surround yourself with a group of people that are getting healthy, and you have to be connected to a community that is doing what you want to do."

—Henry Cloud

"Discussions invariably end on the same note they begin. If you start an argument harshly by attacking your partner, you will end up with at least as much tension as you began with, if not more. Softening (the) startup of your conversations is crucial to resolving relationship conflicts. If your arguments start softly, your relationship is far more likely to be stable and happy."

—www.gottmanblog.com, research by Dr. John Gottman

Jenell Hollett's books and presentations breathe fresh air and hope into our hidden struggles and provide a conduit for open discussion and healing. To schedule the author as a speaker for your business, community, or faith-based event, please visit www.jenellhollett.com

Jenell is pleased to be part of your book club discussion, either by conference call or Web cam. Requests may be sent via email through the author's website.

Also by Jenell Hollett:
What I Learned From Men
A 28-year-old woman uses the lessons she's learned from good men to navigate a major family crisis. As she is forced to move past her old habits of quick judgment and self-indulgence, she realizes the crisis and its effect on her family will permanently change the way she views men, life, and love.

22288347R00130

Made in the USA
San Bernardino, CA
30 June 2015